THE PELICAN SHAKESPEARE

GENERAL EDITOR ALFRED HARBAGE

THE FIRST PART OF

KING HENRY THE FOURTH

WILLIAM SHAKESPEARE

THE FIRST PART OF KING HENRY THE FOURTH

EDITED BY M. A. SHAABER

PENGUIN BOOKS

Penguin Books Ltd, Harmondsworth,
Middlesex, England
Penguin Books, 40 West 23rd Street,
New York, New York 10010, U.S.A.
Penguin Books Australia Ltd, Ringwood,
Victoria, Australia
Penguin Books Canada Limited, 2801 John Street,
Markham, Ontario, Canada L3R 1B4
Penguin Books (N.Z.) Ltd, 182–190 Wairau Road,
Auckland 10, New Zealand

First published in *The Pelican Shakespeare* 1957
This revised edition first published 1970
Reprinted 1974, 1975, 1976, 1978, 1979, 1980 (twice), 1981,
1982, 1983 (twice), 1986, 1987

Library of Congress catalog card number: 73-97747

Printed in the United States of America by
Kingsport Press, Inc., Kingsport, Tennessee
Set in Montoype Ehrhardt

CONTENTS

PUBLISHER'S NOTE

Soon after the thirty-eight volumes forming *The Pelican Shake-speare* had been published, they were brought together in *The Complete Pelican Shakespeare*. The editorial revisions and new textual features are explained in detail in the General Editor's Preface to the one-volume edition. They have all been incorporated in the present volume. The following should be mentioned in particular:

The lines are not numbered in arbitrary units. Instead all lines are numbered which contain a word, phrase, or allusion explained in the glossarial notes. In the occasional instances where there is a long stretch of unannotated text, certain lines are numbered in italics to serve the conventional reference purpose.

The intrusive and often inaccurate place-headings inserted by early editors are omitted (as is becoming standard practise), but for the convenience of those who miss them, an indication of locale now appears as first item in the annotation of each scene.

In the interest of both elegance and utility, each speech-prefix is set in a separate line when the speaker's lines are in verse, except when these words form the second half of a pentameter line. Thus the verse form of the speech is kept visually intact, and turned-over lines are avoided. What is printed as verse and what is printed as prose has, in general, the authority of the original texts. Departures from the original texts in this regard have only the authority of editorial tradition and the judgment of the Pelican editors; and, in a few instances, are admittedly arbitrary.

SHAKESPEARE AND
HIS STAGE

William Shakespeare was christened in Holy Trinity Church, Stratford-upon-Avon, April 26, 1564. His birth is traditionally assigned to April 23. He was the eldest of four boys and two girls who survived infancy in the family of John Shakespeare, glover and trader of Henley Street, and his wife Mary Arden, daughter of a small landowner of Wilmcote. In 1568 John was elected Bailiff (equivalent to Mayor) of Stratford, having already filled the minor municipal offices. The town maintained for the sons of the burgesses a free school, taught by a university graduate and offering preparation in Latin sufficient for university entrance; its early registers are lost, but there can be little doubt that Shakespeare received the formal part of his education in this school.

On November 27, 1582, a license was issued for the marriage of William Shakespeare (aged eighteen) and Ann Hathaway (aged twenty-six), and on May 26, 1583, their child Susanna was christened in Holy Trinity Church. The inference that the marriage was forced upon the youth is natural but not inevitable; betrothal was legally binding at the time, and was sometimes regarded as conferring conjugal rights. Two additional children of the marriage, the twins Hamnet and Judith, were christened on February 2, 1585. Meanwhile the prosperity of the elder Shakespeares had declined, and William was impelled to seek a career outside Stratford.

The tradition that he spent some time as a country

teacher is old but unverifiable. Because of the absence of records his early twenties are called the "lost years," and only one thing about them is certain – that at least some of these years were spent in winning a place in the acting profession. He may have begun as a provincial trouper, but by 1592 he was established in London and prominent enough to be attacked. In a pamphlet of that year, *Groats-worth of Wit*, the ailing Robert Greene complained of the neglect which university writers like himself had suffered from actors, one of whom was daring to set up as a playwright:

. . . an vpstart Crow, beautified with our feathers, that with his *Tygers hart wrapt in a Players hyde*, supposes he is as well able to bombast out a blanke verse as the best of you: and beeing an absolute *Iohannes fac totum*, is in his owne conceit the onely Shake-scene in a countrey.

The pun on his name, and the parody of his line "O tiger's heart wrapped in a woman's hide" (*3 Henry VI*), pointed clearly to Shakespeare. Some of his admirers protested, and Henry Chettle, the editor of Greene's pamphlet, saw fit to apologize:

. . . I am as sory as if the originall fault had beene my fault, because my selfe haue seene his demeanor no lesse ciuill than he excelent in the qualitie he professes: Besides, diuers of worship haue reported his vprightnes of dealing, which argues his honesty, and his facetious grace in writting, that approoues his Art. (Prefatory epistle, *Kind-Harts Dreame*)

The plague closed the London theatres for many months in 1592–94, denying the actors their livelihood. To this period belong Shakespeare's two narrative poems, *Venus and Adonis* and *The Rape of Lucrece*, both dedicated to the Earl of Southampton. No doubt the poet was rewarded with a gift of money as usual in such cases, but he did no further dedicating and we have no reliable information on whether Southampton, or anyone else, became his regular patron. His sonnets, first mentioned in 1598 and published without his consent in 1609, are intimate without being explicitly autobiographical. They seem to commemorate the poet's friendship with an idealized youth, rivalry with a more favored poet, and love affair with a dark mistress; and his bitterness when the mistress betrays him in conjunction with the friend; but it is difficult to decide precisely what the "story" is, impossible to decide whether it is fictional or true. The true distinction of the sonnets, at least of those not purely conventional, rests in the universality of the thoughts and moods they express, and in their poignancy and beauty.

In 1594 was formed the theatrical company known until 1603 as the Lord Chamberlain's men, thereafter as the King's men. Its original membership included, besides Shakespeare, the beloved clown Will Kempe and the famous actor Richard Burbage. The company acted in various London theatres and even toured the provinces, but it is chiefly associated in our minds with the Globe Theatre built on the south bank of the Thames in 1599. Shakespeare was an actor and joint owner of this company (and its Globe) through the remainder of his creative years. His plays, written at the average rate of two a year, together with Burbage's acting won it its place of leadership among the London companies.

Individual plays began to appear in print, in editions both honest and piratical, and the publishers became increasingly aware of the value of Shakespeare's name on the title pages. As early as 1598 he was hailed as the leading English dramatist in the *Palladis Tamia* of Francis Meres:

As *Plautus* and *Seneca* are accounted the best for Comedy and Tragedy among the Latines, so *Shakespeare* among the English is the most excellent in both kinds for the stage: for Comedy, witnes his *Gentlemen of Verona*, his *Errors*, his *Loue labors lost*, his *Loue labours wonne* [at one time in print but no longer extant, at least under this title], his *Midsummers night dream*, & his *Merchant of Venice*; for Tragedy, his *Richard the 2*, *Richard the 3*, *Henry the 4*, *King Iohn*, *Titus Andronicus*, and his *Romeo and Iuliet*.

The note is valuable both in indicating Shakespeare's prestige and in helping us to establish a chronology. In the second half of his writing career, history plays gave place to the great tragedies; and farces and light comedies gave place to the problem plays and symbolic romances. In 1623, seven years after his death, his former fellow-actors, John Heminge and Henry Condell, cooperated with a group of London printers in bringing out his plays in collected form. The volume is generally known as the First Folio.

Shakespeare had never severed his relations with Stratford. His wife and children may sometimes have shared his London lodgings, but their home was Stratford. His son Hamnet was buried there in 1596, and his daughters Susanna and Judith were married there in 1607 and 1616 respectively. (His father, for whom he had secured a coat of arms and thus the privilege of writing himself gentleman, died in 1601, his mother in 1608.) His considerable earnings in London, as actor-sharer, part owner of the Globe, and playwright, were invested chiefly in Stratford property. In 1597 he purchased for £60 New Place, one of the two most imposing residences in the town. A number of other business transactions, as well as minor episodes in his career, have left documentary records. By 1611 he was in a position to retire, and he seems gradually to have withdrawn from theatrical activity in order to live in Stratford. In March, 1616, he made a will, leaving token bequests to Burbage, Heminge, and Condell, but the bulk of his estate to his family. The most famous feature of the will, the bequest of the second-best bed to his wife, reveals nothing about Shakespeare's marriage; the quaintness of the provision seems commonplace to those familiar with ancient testaments. Shakespeare died April 23, 1616, and was buried in the Stratford church where he had been christened. Within seven years a monument was erected to his memory on the north wall of the chancel. Its portrait bust and the Droeshout engraving on the title page of the First Folio provide the only likenesses with an established claim to authenticity. The best verbal vignette was written by his rival Ben Jonson, the more impressive for being imbedded in a context mainly critical :

. . . I loved the man, and doe honour his memory (on this side idolatry) as much as any. Hee was indeed honest, and of an open and free nature: had an excellent Phantsie, brave notions, and gentle expressions. . . . (*Timber or Discoveries*, ca. 1623–30)

*

The reader of Shakespeare's plays is aided by a general knowledge of the way in which they were staged. The King's men acquired a roofed and artificially lighted theatre only toward the close of Shakespeare's career, and then only for winter use. Nearly all his plays were designed for performance in such structures as the Globe – a three-tiered amphitheatre with a large rectangular platform extending to the center of its yard. The plays were staged by daylight, by large casts brilliantly costumed, but with only a minimum of properties, without scenery, and quite possibly without intermissions. There was a rear stage gallery for action "above," and a curtained rear recess for "discoveries" and other special effects, but by far the major portion of any play was enacted upon the projecting platform, with episode following episode in swift succession, and with shifts of time and place signaled the audience only by the momentary clearing of the stage between the episodes. Information about the identity of the characters and, when necessary, about the time and place of the action was incorporated in the dialogue. No place-headings have been inserted in the present editions ; these are apt to obscure the original fluidity of structure, with the emphasis upon action and speech rather than scenic background. (Indications of place are supplied in the footnotes.) The acting, including that of the youthful apprentices to the profession who performed the parts of women, was highly skillful, with a premium placed upon grace of gesture and beauty of diction. The audiences, a cross section of the general public, commonly numbered a thousand, sometimes more than two thousand. Judged by the type of plays they applauded, these audiences were not only large but also perceptive.

THE TEXTS OF THE PLAYS

About half of Shakespeare's plays appeared in print for the first time in the folio volume of 1623. The others had been published individually, usually in quarto volumes, during his lifetime or in the six years following his death. The copy used by the printers of the quartos varied greatly in merit, sometimes representing Shakespeare's true text, sometimes only a debased version of that text. The copy used by the printers of the folio also varied in merit, but was chosen with care. Since it consisted of the best available manuscripts, or the more acceptable quartos (although frequently in editions other than the first), or of quartos corrected by reference to manuscripts, we have good or reasonably good texts of most of the thirty-seven plays.

In the present series, the plays have been newly edited from quarto or folio texts, depending, when a choice offered, upon which is now regarded by bibliographical specialists as the more authoritative. The ideal has been to reproduce the chosen texts with as few alterations as possible, beyond occasional relineation, expansion of abbreviations, and modernization of punctuation and spelling. Emendation is held to a minimum, and such material as has been added, in the way of stage directions and lines supplied by an alternative text, has been enclosed in square brackets.

None of the plays printed in Shakespeare's lifetime were divided into acts and scenes, and the inference is that the author's own manuscripts were not so divided. In the folio collection, some of the plays remained undivided, some were divided into acts, and some were divided into acts and scenes. During the eighteenth century all of the plays were divided into acts and scenes, and in the Cambridge edition of the mid-nineteenth century, from which the influential Globe text derived, this division was more or less regularized and the lines were numbered. Many useful works of reference employ the act–scene–line apparatus thus established.

Since this act–scene division is obviously convenient, but is of very dubious authority so far as Shakespeare's own structural principles are concerned, or the original manner of staging his plays, a problem is presented to modern editors. In the present series the act–scene division is retained marginally, and may be viewed as a reference aid like the line numbering. A star marks the points of division when these points have been determined by a cleared stage indicating a shift of time and place in the action of the play, or when no harm results from the editorial assumption that there is such a shift. However, at those points where the established division is clearly misleading – that is, where continuous action has been split up into separate "scenes" – the star is omitted and the distortion corrected. This mechanical expedient seemed the best means of combining utility and accuracy.

THE GENERAL EDITOR

INTRODUCTION

Shakespeare wrote *1 Henry IV* soon after *Richard II*. The plays are closely linked: *1 Henry IV* begins very soon after the end of *Richard II* and often refers to the events of that play; anticipations of *1 Henry IV* are planted in *Richard II*. As *Richard II* was written by 1596, the likely date for *1 Henry IV* is 1597.

Although the play was called *The History of Henry IV* in all the early printings beginning with the quarto of 1598 (it was differentiated from the second part only when the two were first printed together in the folio of 1623), it is not chiefly concerned with King Henry IV, and when he wrote it Shakespeare evidently had other interests in mind. As he followed it up with *2 Henry IV* and *Henry V*, it may seem that his idea was to write a series of plays on the ultimate origins of the Wars of the Roses similar to the series on these wars – the three parts of *Henry VI* and *Richard III* – which he had written more than five years earlier. But though the ultimate origins of the rivalry of Lancaster and York are to be found in the deposition of Richard II, the dire effects prophesied by the Bishop of Carlisle (*Richard II*, IV, i) were long postponed and fighting did not break out for almost half a century. Over this interval loomed the heroic figure of Henry of Monmouth, the savior of his country (or at least his father's reign) as Prince of Wales, the conqueror of France as King Henry V, who while he lived averted the consequences of disaffection. He is the theme of the two *Henry IV* plays and of *Henry V*. Moreover, it is a story with a triumphant, not a tragic, outcome, and it required a different mode of treatment from *Richard II*.

The real center of *1 Henry IV*, the only character active in all the elements of the plot, is Prince Hal. Shakespeare's decision to present him in two plays* rather than one must have grown out of the curious legend of the prince's wild youth that he found in the histories. These credited the victor of Agincourt, the most Christian of the medieval kings of England, with an unruly and profligate youth, spent in dissolute company, which, however, he shed like a coat the moment he was called upon to rule. The first phase of this astonishing development is the subject of this play; it is the prelude to the revelation of Henry V in all his glory.

Though the contrast between the truant prince and the glorious king is kept before us in this play, just as it is in *Henry V*, it is a contrast of appearances rather than realities. To Shakespeare the prince is the same man potentially as the king. The discrepancy is not between a bad prince and a good king but between the prince's true nature and his reputation, between what he will be when called upon to assert himself and what he seems to be while idly, even basely, biding his time. There is no real reformation: the prince always knows what is right and prefers it; only appearances are against him. To reconcile this discrepancy Shakespeare resorted to a most unpsychological explanation, that the prince was deliberately waiting for the best opportunity to show the stuff he was made of, but evidently he thought it sufficient. Actually the play, by implication, gives a much better reason – that the prince was enjoying Falstaff – and this reason spectators at the play cordially accept.

---

* *1 Henry IV* and *Henry V*: to the present editor it seems more likely than not that *2 Henry IV* is an unpremeditated sequel to the first part, supplying the demand for more Falstaff.

The play, then, is a true story expanded and given additional dramatic force by the playwright's art. Much of it is based on the chronicler Holinshed's account of the reigns of Henry IV and Henry V. Shakespeare had also read the earlier chronicle of Hall (with whose story Holinshed's for the most part coincides) and Samuel Daniel's poem, *The Civil Wars* (1595), which magnifies the part of the prince in the battle of Shrewsbury and suggests his combat with Hotspur. An old play called *The Famous Victories of Henry V* had already covered the ground, beginning with the robbery on Gad's Hill and ending with the French marriage. As it is known to us only from an abbreviated and garbled version printed in 1598, it is hard to say how much Shakespeare, who presumably knew the authentic version of it, drew from it. But Shakespeare was not a historian but a playwright and his task was not to reproduce history but to transform it into drama. When good drama and history happened to coincide, he would give a faithful enough account of history as his informants had recorded it; when history proved recalcitrant to dramatization, he would ignore it or remold it to serve his purpose. As a result the play combines details perfectly true with others wholly imaginary. In a manner of speaking, the former warrant the latter. Shakespeare remembers that Bolingbroke landed at Ravenspurgh, swore an oath at Doncaster, and met Hotspur at Berkeley Castle; when he makes the king older than he really was and Hotspur younger it is not out of ignorance but out of a sense of what will make his play more effective. With the playwright's instinct for compressed and continuous action, he suppresses all indications of intervals of time between the successive episodes of the story, so that everything seems to happen in a few weeks, though actually a year elapsed between the defeat of Mortimer (June 22, 1402) and the battle of Shrewsbury (July 21, 1403). When history is silent, failing to explain why the prince played the madcap, what form his pranks took, what kind of man Hotspur really was, Shakespeare falls back on his invention. Occasionally history misled him: Holinshed confused the Sir Edmund Mortimer who married Glendower's daughter with his nephew Edmund Mortimer, fifth earl of March, who was proclaimed heir to the throne by Richard II in 1398, and Shakespeare followed.

The structure of the play is simple and the plot moves somewhat slowly. In the early scenes three oppositions are lined up: that of the rebels and the king and the loyal party, that of Hotspur and the prince, that of the prince's bad reputation and truant disposition and his actual sterling worth. All these are to be resolved on the battlefield of Shrewsbury and the play has little to do but march undeviatingly toward that final arbitrement. Successive scenes showing one or another of these opposed forces advancing towards the day of decision sharpen the oppositions. As the battle approaches, the alternating scenes become shorter and the various oppositions tend to merge. The events of the battle answer all questions: loyalty triumphs over disaffection, Hal over Hotspur, and the prince's valor and fidelity over all suspicions.

This simple plot (lacking the fresh complications and changes of alignment which make the plot of *Richard III* more exciting) is, however, greatly enlivened by the skill with which individual scenes are developed. The story of the robbery on Gad's Hill, a series of scenes which might be called a subplot if it did not come to an end before the play is half over, obviously gathers momentum as it develops and reaches its own peculiar climax. Some scenes are planned like miniature dramas. A good example is the scene at Glendower's house. It is useful to the plot only so far as it shows the rebels forging ahead with their preparations and wickedly planning to divide England. Shakespeare imposes dramatic form upon it by working up a temperamental antagonism between Hotspur and Glendower which reaches a high pitch a moment before Glendower backs down. The advantage which Hotspur gains thereby – it is not very great, for it lets him in for a dressing-down by Mortimer and Worcester – is short-lived, for presently Glendower takes the wind out of his sails by producing the supernatural music he had promised. The occasion of this music is brought about by the development of a contrast between the sentimental Mortimers, those odd victims of the barrier of language, and the unsentimental Percies. The scene is full of dramatic tension peculiar to itself and attains something like a dramatic resolution before it is over. The second tavern scene and the scene between the king and the prince also contain complete reversals of the situation presented at the outset.

The opposition of the Percies to the king, the historical backbone of the play, is no doubt a simple struggle for power, but dramatically at least it is a little more than that, for the whole is tinged with irony because of the king's equivocal claim to the throne and his consciousness of the instability of his position. The picture of him – old, shaken, and wan with care – is dramatic, not historical; he was actually a vigorous man in his middle thirties. He hankers after going on a crusade to expiate the wrong he did King Richard; he looks upon the prince's recalcitrance as a "rod of heaven" to punish his "mistreadings." The ambiguousness of his conduct – his determination to hold on to the prize he has gained and his twinges of conscience – is never resolved; he is more impressive and sounds deeper notes because he is never unequivocally presented as either the "vile politician" that Hotspur thinks he is or as something else.

The rivalry of the prince and Hotspur is the dramatic mainspring of the play: the stroke that kills the latter awards the palm of supremacy to the prince, checks rebellion, and confirms the prince's loyalty to his father. This antagonism is announced in the first scene of the play and kept alive, in one way or another, in almost every other. It is pure invention. Far from being a "northern youth," Hotspur was older than the prince's father, and, though he was certainly killed at Shrewsbury, nobody knows who killed him. Shakespeare undoubtedly strove to make the prince seem the better man. Hotspur's uncertain temper is emphasized in every scene in which he appears. His intractability is deplored by his father and his uncle (I, iii) and by his wife (II, iii); the prince's travesty of his daily routine of killing some six or seven dozen of Scots at a breakfast is a shrewd stroke. Worcester and Vernon question his leadership (IV, iii). His impatience of any praise of his adversary is twice underscored. His valedictory on the eve of the battle is a curious combination of bravado and fatalism. The crowning touch is added to his infatuation in the scene in which he partitions England and cavils at the details of the partition: obviously there is no sympathy for one who would dismember his native country. On the other hand, the prince is justified at every point. We are assured of his essential sobriety and dependability in the soliloquy he speaks at the end of the first scene in which he appears. The odium of his wild oats is transferred to Falstaff and dissolves in laughter. At the midpoint of the play he assures his father that he is true blue in spite of appearances, and though promise is not performance, performance follows in due course. He does full justice to Hotspur's prowess and reputation. His enemies testify to his valor and modesty (IV, i, 97 ff.; V, ii, 51 ff.). And on the day of decision he redeems his lost opinion triumphantly.

Yet all this careful weighting of the scales has often gone for nothing. Readers and spectators in the theatre become partisans of Hotspur and wish to reverse the verdict. Hotspur's disloyalty to the country he would divide out of selfish ambition is overlooked: we have a sneaking sympathy for rebels, especially in fiction. The prince is put down as a hypocrite because his cloaking of his right royal nature is the result of calculation – as if calculation were not the duty of a reasonable man and impulsive conduct a form of disorder. His later offenses, his rejection of Falstaff in 2 *Henry IV* and his sanctimoniousness in *Henry V*, are made retroactive and added to the indictment. The real cause of this reversal of the verdict is, however, dramatic: Hotspur's part is aggressive and dynamic throughout while the prince must be kept under wraps till almost the end. The advantage to the actor who plays Hotspur, and the disadvantage to the actor who plays the prince, is enormous. Hotspur is by far the best acting part in the historical action of the play; he dazzles us so thoroughly as to disarm criticism. Since this is so, Shakespeare cannot escape responsibility, but in his defense it may be said that he has put up plenty of signposts to show which way our sympathies should take.

But even Hotspur is overshadowed by Falstaff, who is indeed the great triumph of this play. Otherwise a superior battle-piece, it is transfigured by his presence into something unique and transcendent. Falstaff was made out of whole cloth. There is a character corresponding to him in *The Famous Victories*, but even if his part in that play as Shakespeare knew it was much more amusing than it is in the version we know, it hardly seems likely that he afforded Shakespeare more than a start. Nothing that history tells about either the Lollard martyr Sir John Oldcastle (as Falstaff was called in the earliest performances, before the name was changed out of deference to the displeasure of his living descendants) or Sir John Fastolfe (*1 Henry VI*, III, ii; IV, i) accounts for the immortal character that Shakespeare made. Falstaff is fitted to the role designed for him with the greatest adroitness. He becomes the embodiment of the prince's wild oats. The prince really does little or nothing reprehensible: he takes part in the robbery, but his character is carefully safeguarded from the start and he restores the money with advantage; otherwise he only gets a little tipsy, plays a poor practical joke on the drawer, and exchanges vituperation with Falstaff. It is Falstaff who creates the atmosphere of depravity, the prince sharing in it but not responsible for it and always standing somewhat apart from it. Falstaff is a kind of scapegoat: he takes upon him the vices which legend imputed to the prince. Further to exculpate the prince, the sting is extracted from these vices by presenting them only in the element of laughter, the infallible solvent of morality. Only the sternest self-control enables us to remember, as we laugh at Falstaff's drollery, that he is really a liar, a sponger, a glutton, a drunkard, a thief, and much more that we must disapprove of. As insulation for the prince's character, Falstaff is a superb dramatic invention.

Traditionally a comic character is the butt of ridicule, a simpleton, a monomaniac, or an impostor who, like that other Falstaff who swaggers through *The Merry Wives of Windsor*, overreaches himself in the end and is exposed to the derisive laughter of men of better judgment. But the Falstaff of this play, for all the verbal derision hurled at him by the prince and others, which he always parries skillfully enough, is never completely exposed, discomfited, or humiliated by the turn of events; he always manages to earn at least a draw and often something like a triumph. At the end of the play he is even left in dubious possession of the claim of victory over Hotspur. For success like this we have no derision; indeed, at least in fiction, it excites something much more like sympathy, and Falstaff carries away our admiration, or at least our astonishment, by his overwhelming effrontery. When we laugh with him we forfeit all chance of sitting in judgment upon him. The utter disabling of our normal censoriousness, the assigning to Falstaff of a role that is sympathetic as well as depraved, is indeed a triumph of the comic imagination.

Moreover, the equivocal Falstaff is the essential Falstaff. He is never twice quite the same; he is a series of impersonations. He is an inveterate comic actor and every man is a stooge who must play up to him. His parts are without number and every one is followed by its opposite: the old man and the frisky youth, the fat man and the active man (or at least a simulacrum thereof), the sponger and the lordly patron (of Bardolph and the likes of him), the libertine and the critic of manners (whose ruminations on the ways of the world are heavily flavored with biblical phraseology), the soldier and the coward – or at least the propounder of the axiom that the better part of valor is discretion. Of all his parts the most famous is that of the artful dodger: at least three times he is backed into a corner, only to wriggle out by a triumphant equivocation (he was a coward on instinct, the prince owes him his love and his love is worth a million, he gave Hotspur a wound in the thigh). Of all his parts the most surprising is that of debunker of honor: the soliloquy in which he proves it only a word might seem to undermine the whole basis of the serious parts of the play, but by that time we are so used to Falstaff's "wrenching the true cause the false way" that we take it as another piece of pseudo-logic like his argument that robbery is no sin if it is a man's vocation. His protean character makes the wrangle over his cowardice, which literary critics have been carrying on for a hundred and fifty years now, seem irrelevant. Of course Falstaff is a coward when he runs away or shams death; a brave man running away or playing dead would not be funny. But at the same time the complete aplomb with which he carries off these pieces of "discretion," utterly different from the teeth-chattering and knee-knocking of the craven coward, makes him a coward different from all others and much funnier. The laughter that greets Falstaff's sallies, so far as it is more than merely a tribute to his wit, is a delighted recognition of the adroitness with which he is always pretending to be something that we know he is not or at least was not a minute, an hour, or a day ago. His bright eye, his rum-soaked voice, and his unwieldy bulk dominate every situation in which he finds himself and he turns them all into mirth by assuming whatever part one would least expect of him. He blows through the play like a great gust of laughter and comes within an ace of turning Shakespeare's history of Henry IV into the comedy of Falstaff.

University of Pennsylvania   M. A. SHAABER

NOTE ON THE TEXT

The present text follows, with only a few emendations, that of the first quarto (1598), which is believed to have been printed from the author's draft. In the folio text of 1623, printed from the fifth quarto (1613), the play was first divided into acts and scenes. The act–scene division supplied marginally in the present text is that of the folio except that V, ii of the folio is divided into two scenes. Below are listed all substantive departures from the quarto text, with the adopted reading in italics followed by the quarto reading in roman. The letters Q0 represent a quarto of which only four leaves survive. It was probably published in 1598 and served as copy for Q1.

I, i, 30 *Therefor* (ed.) Therefore   62 *a dear* (Q5) deere   69 *blood* (Q5) bloud.

I, ii, 30–31 *moon. . . . proof now :* (Rowe) moone, . . . proofe. Now   74 *similes* (Q5) smiles   106 *Sugar? Jack,* (Capell) Sugar Iacke ?   117 *Gad's Hill* (Wilson) Gadshill   148 *thou* (Pope) the   152 *Bardolph* (Theobald) Haruey   *Peto* (Dering) Rossill

I, iii, 96 *tongue* (Hanmer) tongue: 139 *struck* (Malone) strooke   201 *Hotspur* (Q5) Omitted (Q1)   254 *for I* (F) I   262 *granted. . . . lord,* (Thirlby) granted . . . Lord.   290 *course.* (Johnson) course.

II, i, 32 *1. Carrier* (Hanmer) Car.   71 *foot land-rakers* (Hanmer) footlande rakers

II, ii, 16 *two-and-twenty* (F) xxii   20 (and throughout the play) *Bardolph* (F) Bardoll (or Bardol)   40 *Go hang* (Q3) Hang   48 *Bardolph. What* (Johnson) Bardoll, what   49 *Gadshill* (Johnson) Bar.   78 *Ah* (Rowe) a   102 *fat rogue* (Q0) rogue

II, iii, 4 *In respect* (Q6) in the respect   45 *thee* (Q2) the   66 *A roan* (Q3) Roane

23

II, iv, 31 *precedent* (President F) present 114 *(pitiful-hearted Titan!)* (Warburton) pittiful harted titan 164 *Prince* (Dering) Gads. 165, 167, 171 *Gadshill* (F) Ross. 232 *eel-skin* (Hanmer) elsskin 288 *Tell* (F) Faith tell 324 *Owen* (Dering) Ω 375 *tristful* (Dering) trustfull 431 *reverend* (F) reverent 450 *lean* (Q2) lane 468 *mad* (F3) made 510 *Peto* (F) Omitted (Q) 514 *Prince* (F) Omitted (Q)

III, i, 100 *cantle* (F) scantle 116 *I will* (Pope) I'le 128 *metre* (F) miter 131 *on* (Q3) an 261 *hot* (F) Hot.

III, ii, 110 *capital* (Q2) capitall.

III, iii, 32 *that's* (Q3) that 35 *Gad's Hill* (Wilson) Gadshill 54 *tithe* (Theobald) tight 71 *four-and-twenty* (F) xxiiii. 113 *no thing* (Q3) nothing 165 *guests* (Q2) ghesse 168 *court.* (Keightley) court 181 *two-and-twenty* (F) xxii. 191 *o'clock* (Q2) of clocke

IV, i, 20 *lord* (Capell) mind 55 *Is* (F) tis 108 *dropped* (Q2) drop 116 *altar* (Q4) altars 126 *cannot* (Q5) can 127 *yet* (Q5) it

IV, ii, 3 *Sutton Co'fil'* (Cambridge eds) Sutton cophill

IV, iii, 21 *horse* (Q5) horses 28 *ours* (Q6) our 72 *heirs as pages,* (Singer) heires, as Pages 82 *country's* (Q5) Countrey

V, i, 25 *I do* (F) I 131 *then?* (Q2) then 137 *will it* (Q2) wil

V, ii, 3 *undone* (Q5) vnder one 10 *ne'er* (F) neuer 70 *Upon* (Pope) On

V, iii, 22 *A* (Capell) Ah 39 *stand'st* (Q2) stands 50 *get'st* (Q2) gets

V, iv, 33 *So* (F) and 67 *Nor* (F) Now 91 *thee* (Q7) the 155 *ours* (Q2) our 156 *let's* (Q4) let us

V, v, 36 *bend you* (Q4) bend, you

24

THE FIRST PART
OF KING HENRY
THE FOURTH

King Henry the Fourth
Henry, Prince of Wales ⎱
Prince John of Lancaster ⎰ the King's sons
Earl of Westmoreland
Sir Walter Blunt
Thomas Percy, Earl of Worcester
Henry Percy, Earl of Northumberland
Henry Percy ('Hotspur'), his son
Edmund Mortimer, Earl of March
Richard Scroop, Archbishop of York
Archibald, Earl of Douglas
Owen Glendower
Sir Richard Vernon
Sir John Falstaff
Sir Michael, a friend of the Archbishop of York
Poins
Gadshill
Peto
Bardolph
Vintner of an Eastcheap Tavern
Francis, a waiter
Chamberlain of an inn at Rochester
Ostler
Mugs and another Carrier
Travellers on the road from Rochester to London
Sheriff
Hotspur's Servant
Messenger from Northumberland
Two Messengers (soldiers in Hotspur's army)
Lady Percy, Hotspur's wife and Mortimer's sister
Lady Mortimer, Glendower's daughter
Mistress Quickly, hostess of an Eastcheap Tavern

Scene: *England and Wales*]

THE FIRST PART
OF KING HENRY
THE FOURTH

Enter the King, Lord John of Lancaster, Earl of   I, i
Westmoreland, [Sir Walter Blunt,] with others.

KING

So shaken as we are, so wan with care,
Find we a time for frighted peace to pant   2
And breathe short-winded accents of new broils   3
To be commenced in stronds afar remote.   4
No more the thirsty entrance of this soil   5
Shall daub her lips with her own children's blood:
No more shall trenching war channel her fields,   7
Nor bruise her flow'rets with the armèd hoofs
Of hostile paces. Those opposèd eyes
Which, like the meteors of a troubled heaven,   10
All of one nature, of one substance bred,
Did lately meet in the intestine shock
And furious close of civil butchery,   13
Shall now in mutual well-beseeming ranks
March all one way and be no more opposed
Against acquaintance, kindred, and allies.
The edge of war, like an ill-sheathèd knife,
No more shall cut his master. Therefore, friends,   18
As far as to the sepulchre of Christ –

I, i The Court of King Henry IV   2 *Find we* let us find   3 *accents* words
4 *stronds* strands, shores   5 *entrance* fissures (through which moisture is
absorbed)   7 *trenching* cutting; *channel* cut furrows in   10 *meteors* atmos-
pheric disturbances (perhaps a thunderstorm)   13 *close* hand-to-hand
fighting   18 *his* its

Whose soldier now, under whose blessèd cross
We are impressèd and engaged to fight –
22   Forthwith a power of English shall we levy,
Whose arms were moulded in their mother's womb
To chase these pagans in those holy fields
Over whose acres walked those blessèd feet
Which fourteen hundred years ago were nailed
For our advantage on the bitter cross.
But this our purpose now is twelve month old,
29   And bootless 'tis to tell you we will go.
Therefor we meet not now. Then let me hear
31   Of you, my gentle cousin Westmoreland,
What yesternight our council did decree
33   In forwarding this dear expedience.

WESTMORELAND
34   My liege, this haste was hot in question
35   And many limits of the charge set down
36   But yesternight; when all athwart there came
37   A post from Wales, loaden with heavy news,
Whose worst was that the noble Mortimer,
Leading the men of Herefordshire to fight
Against the irregular and wild Glendower,
Was by the rude hands of that Welshman taken,
A thousand of his people butcherèd;
43   Upon whose dead corpse there was such misuse,
44   Such beastly shameless transformation,
By those Welshwomen done as may not be
Without much shame retold or spoken of.

KING
It seems then that the tidings of this broil
Brake off our business for the Holy Land.

---

22 *power* army   **29** *bootless* useless   **31** *cousin* form of address (no kinship implied)   **33** *dear expedience* important expedition   **34** *liege* feudal superior; *hot in question* warmly debated   **35** *limits . . . charge* assignments of responsibility   **36** *athwart* contrarily   **37** *post* messenger; *heavy* depressing   **43** *corpse* corpses   **44** *transformation* i.e. mutilation

WESTMORELAND

   This, matched with other, did, my gracious lord;   49
   For more uneven and unwelcome news   50
   Came from the north, and thus it did import:
   On Holy-rood Day the gallant Hotspur there,
   Young Harry Percy, and brave Archibald,
   That ever-valiant and approvèd Scot,   54
   At Holmedon met,   55
   Where they did spend a sad and bloody hour;
   As by discharge of their artillery   57
   And shape of likelihood the news was told;
   For he that brought them, in the very heat   59
   And pride of their contention did take horse,   60
   Uncertain of the issue any way.

KING

   Here is a dear, a true-industrious friend,
   Sir Walter Blunt, new lighted from his horse,
   Stained with the variation of each soil
   Betwixt that Holmedon and this seat of ours,
   And he hath brought us smooth and welcome news.
   The Earl of Douglas is discomfited;
   Ten thousand bold Scots, two-and-twenty knights,
   Balked in their own blood did Sir Walter see   69
   On Holmedon's plains. Of prisoners, Hotspur took
   Mordake Earl of Fife and eldest son   71
   To beaten Douglas, and the Earl of Athol,
   Of Murray, Angus, and Menteith.
   And is not this an honourable spoil?
   A gallant prize? Ha, cousin, is it not?

WESTMORELAND

   In faith,

---

49 *other* others, other tidings 50 *uneven* disconcerting 54 *approvèd* of
proved valor 55 *Holmedon* Humbleton in Northumberland 57–58 *by . . .
shape of likelihood* according to . . . probability 59 *them* news 60 *pride*
height 69 *Balked* (1) heaped up, (2) defeated 71 *Mordake* i.e. Murdoch
(actually son of the Duke of Albany)

It is a conquest for a prince to boast of.

KING
Yea, there thou mak'st me sad, and mak'st me sin
In envy that my Lord Northumberland
Should be the father to so blest a son –
A son who is the theme of honor's tongue,
Amongst a grove the very straightest plant;
83   Who is sweet fortune's minion and her pride;
Whilst I, by looking on the praise of him,
See riot and dishonor stain the brow
Of my young Harry. O that it could be proved
That some night-tripping fairy had exchanged
In cradle clothes our children where they lay,
89   And called mine Percy, his Plantagenet!
90   Then would I have his Harry, and he mine.
91   But let him from my thoughts. What think you, coz,
Of this young Percy's pride? The prisoners
Which he in this adventure hath surprised
94   To his own use he keeps, and sends me word
I shall have none but Mordake Earl of Fife.

WESTMORELAND
This is his uncle's teaching, this is Worcester,
97   Malevolent to you in all aspects,
98   Which makes him prune himself and bristle up
The crest of youth against your dignity.

KING
But I have sent for him to answer this;
And for this cause awhile we must neglect
Our holy purpose to Jerusalem.
Cousin, on Wednesday next our council we
Will hold at Windsor. So inform the lords;
But come yourself with speed to us again;

---

83 *minion* favorite   89 *Plantagenet* family name of the kings descended
from Henry II   90 *would I have* I would demand   91 *let him* let him go;
coz cousin   94 *To . . . use* i.e. to collect their ransoms   97 *aspects* (literally)
positions of a star   98 *prune* preen

For more is to be said and to be done
Than out of anger can be utterèd.
WESTMORELAND
I will, my liege.   *Exeunt.*

                               *

Enter Prince of Wales and Sir John Falstaff.   I, ii
FALSTAFF Now, Hal, what time of day is it, lad?   1
PRINCE Thou art so fat-witted with drinking of old sack, 2
   and unbuttoning thee after supper, and sleeping upon
   benches after noon, that thou hast forgotten to demand 4
   that truly which thou wouldest truly know. What a devil 5
   hast thou to do with the time of the day? Unless hours
   were cups of sack, and minutes capons, and clocks the
   tongues of bawds, and dials the signs of leaping houses, 8
   and the blessed sun himself a fair hot wench in flame-
   colored taffeta, I see no reason why thou shouldst be so 10
   superfluous to demand the time of the day.
FALSTAFF Indeed you come near me now, Hal; for we that 12
   take purses go by the moon and the seven stars, and not by 13
   Phoebus, he, that wand'ring knight so fair. And I 14
   prithee, sweet wag, when thou art a king, as, God save
   thy grace – majesty I should say, for grace thou wilt 16
   have none –
PRINCE What, none?
FALSTAFF No, by my troth; not so much as will serve to 18
   be prologue to an egg and butter.   19
PRINCE Well, how then? Come, roundly, roundly.   20

I, ii An apartment of the Prince? 1 *what . . . it* (implies doubt that the
person addressed is bright enough to know what time it is) 2 *sack* Spanish
white wine 4 *benches* privy-seats 5 *truly* correctly 8 *dials* clocks 10–11
be . . . demand allow yourself the luxury of demanding 12 *you . . . now* i.e.
you have me there 13 *go* (1) count time, (2) walk; *seven stars* Big Dipper
14 *Phoebus* the sun; *wand'ring knight* knight errant (suggested by the Knight
of the Sun, the hero of a romance called *The Mirror of Knighthood*) 16 *thy
grace* used, like 'your majesty,' in addressing royalty; *grace* virtuous
motives 18 *troth* faith 19 *egg and butter* a mere snack, requiring only a
short grace 20 *roundly* without beating about the bush

21 FALSTAFF Marry, then, sweet wag, when thou art king,
22   let not us that are squires of the night's body be called
23   thieves of the day's beauty. Let us be Diana's foresters,
     gentlemen of the shade, minions of the moon; and let
25   men say we be men of good government, being
     governed as the sea is, by our noble and chaste mistress
27   the moon, under whose countenance we steal.
28 PRINCE Thou sayest well, and it holds well too; for the
     fortune of us that are the moon's men doth ebb and flow
     like the sea, being governed, as the sea is, by the moon.
     As, for proof now: a purse of gold most resolutely
     snatched on Monday night and most dissolutely spent
33   on Tuesday morning; got with swearing 'Lay by,' and
     spent with crying 'Bring in'; now in as low an ebb as the
35   foot of the ladder, and by-and-by in as high a flow as the
     ridge of the gallows.
   FALSTAFF By the Lord, thou say'st true, lad – and is not
     my hostess of the tavern a most sweet wench?
39 PRINCE As the honey of Hybla, my old lad of the castle –
40   and is not a buff jerkin a most sweet robe of durance?
   FALSTAFF How now, how now, mad wag? What, in thy
42   quips and thy quiddities? What a plague have I to do
     with a buff jerkin?
44 PRINCE Why, what a pox have I to do with my hostess of
     the tavern?
46 FALSTAFF Well, thou hast called her to a reckoning many
     a time and oft.
   PRINCE Did I ever call for thee to pay thy part?

---

21 *Marry* well, indeed   22 *squires* body-servants   23 *thieves . . . beauty*
idlers by day; *Diana's foresters* i.e. a better-sounding name than 'thieves'
25 *government* conduct   27 *countenance* (1) face, (2) patronage; *steal* (1)
rob, (2) walk stealthily   28 *it holds well* the comparison is appropriate   33
Lay by put down your weapons   35 *ladder* that from the platform to the
ridge of the gallows, climbed by the culprit   39 *Hybla* place in Sicily
famous for honey; *old . . . castle* (1) roisterer, (2) Oldcastle   40 *buff jerkin*
leather jacket; *durance* (1) kind of durable cloth, (2) imprisonment   42
quiddities hair-splittings   44 *pox* syphilis   46 *reckoning* settlement (of the
bill)

FALSTAFF No; I'll give thee thy due, thou hast paid all there.

PRINCE Yea, and elsewhere, so far as my coin would stretch; and where it would not, I have used my credit.

FALSTAFF Yea, and so used it that, were it not here apparent that thou art heir apparent – But I prithee, sweet wag, shall there be gallows standing in England when thou art king? and resolution thus fubbed as it is 55 with the rusty curb of old father antic the law? Do not 56 thou, when thou art king, hang a thief.

PRINCE No; thou shalt.

FALSTAFF Shall I? O rare! By the Lord, I'll be a brave 59 judge.

PRINCE Thou judgest false already. I mean, thou shalt have the hanging of the thieves and so become a rare hangman.

FALSTAFF Well, Hal, well; and in some sort it jumps with 64 my humor as well as waiting in the court, I can tell you. 65

PRINCE For obtaining of suits? 66

FALSTAFF Yea, for obtaining of suits, whereof the hangman hath no lean wardrobe. 'Sblood, I am as melan- 68 choly as a gib-cat or a lugged bear. 69

PRINCE Or an old lion, or a lover's lute.

FALSTAFF Yea, or the drone of a Lincolnshire bagpipe. 71

PRINCE What sayest thou to a hare, or the melancholy of 72 Moor Ditch? 73

FALSTAFF Thou hast the most unsavory similes, and art indeed the most comparative, rascalliest, sweet young 75 prince. But, Hal, I prithee trouble me no more with vanity. I would to God thou and I knew where a 77

---

55 *resolution* courage; *fubbed* thwarted   56 *antic* buffoon   59 *brave* splendid   64 *jumps with* suits   65 *waiting* being in attendance; *court* i.e. the royal court   66 *suits* petitions   68 *wardrobe* the clothes of those he hangs are the hangman's perquisite; *'Sblood* by God's blood   69 *gib-cat* tomcat; *lugged* baited   71 *drone* bass pipe   72 *hare* proverbially melancholy   73 *Moor Ditch* an open sewer   75 *comparative* abusive   77 *vanity* worldliness

78   commodity of good names were to be bought. An old
79   lord of the council rated me the other day in the street
about you, sir, but I marked him not; and yet he talked
very wisely, but I regarded him not; and yet he talked
wisely, and in the street too.

83 PRINCE Thou didst well, for wisdom cries out in the
streets, and no man regards it.

85 FALSTAFF O, thou hast damnable iteration, and art indeed
able to corrupt a saint. Thou hast done much harm
upon me, Hal – God forgive thee for it! Before I knew
88   thee, Hal, I knew nothing; and now am I, if a man
should speak truly, little better than one of the wicked. I
must give over this life, and I will give it over! By the
91   Lord, an I do not, I am a villain! I'll be damned for
never a king's son in Christendom.

PRINCE Where shall we take a purse to-morrow, Jack?

94 FALSTAFF Zounds, where thou wilt, lad! I'll make one.
95   An I do not, call me villain and baffle me.

PRINCE I see a good amendment of life in thee – from
praying to purse-taking.

FALSTAFF Why, Hal, 'tis my vocation, Hal. 'Tis no sin
for a man to labor in his vocation.

    Enter Poins.

100   Poins! Now shall we know if Gadshill have set a match.
101   O, if men were to be saved by merit, what hole in hell
102   were hot enough for him? This is the most omnipotent
103   villain that ever cried 'stand!' to a true man.

104 PRINCE Good morrow, Ned.

POINS Good morrow, sweet Hal. What says Monsieur

---

78 *commodity* lot   79 *rated* rebuked   83–84 *wisdom . . . regards it* 'Wisdom
crieth without; she uttereth her voice in the streets. She crieth . . . saying,
". . . I have stretched out my hand, and no man regarded"' (Proverbs i,
20–24)   85 *iteration* repetition (of scriptural texts)   88 *knew nothing* was
innocent   91 *an* if; *villain* the opposite of a gentleman   94 *Zounds* by
God's wounds; *make one* be one of the party   95 *baffle* degrade   100 *set a
match* made arrangements (for a holdup)   101 *saved by merit* i.e. as they are
not: they are saved by grace   102 *omnipotent* complete   103 *stand* i.e.
hands up; *true* honest   104 *morrow* morning

Remorse? What says Sir John Sack and Sugar? Jack, how agrees the devil and thee about thy soul, that thou soldest him on Good Friday last for a cup of Madeira and a cold capon's leg?

PRINCE Sir John stands to his word, the devil shall have 110 his bargain; for he was never yet a breaker of proverbs. He will give the devil his due. 112

POINS Then art thou damned for keeping thy word with the devil.

PRINCE Else he had been damned for cozening the devil. 115

POINS But, my lads, my lads, to-morrow morning, by four o'clock early, at Gad's Hill! There are pilgrims 117 going to Canterbury with rich offerings, and traders riding to London with fat purses. I have vizards for you 119 all; you have horses for yourselves. Gadshill lies to- 120 night in Rochester. I have bespoke supper to-morrow night in Eastcheap. We may do it as secure as sleep. If you will go, I will stuff your purses full of crowns; if you will not, tarry at home and be hanged!

FALSTAFF Hear ye, Yedward: if I tarry at home and go not, I'll hang you for going.

POINS You will, chops? 127

FALSTAFF Hal, wilt thou make one?

PRINCE Who, I rob? I a thief? Not I, by my faith.

FALSTAFF There's neither honesty, manhood, nor good fellowship in thee, nor thou cam'st not of the blood royal if thou darest not stand for ten shillings. 132

PRINCE Well then, once in my days I'll be a madcap.

FALSTAFF Why, that's well said.

PRINCE Well, come what will, I'll tarry at home.

FALSTAFF By the Lord, I'll be a traitor then, when thou art king.

PRINCE I care not.

---

110 *stands to* i.e. is as good as   112 *his due* i.e. Falstaff's soul   115 *cozening* cheating   117 *Gad's Hill* on the road from Canterbury to London   119 *vizards* masks   120 *lies* lodges   126 *chops* fat-cheeks   132 *stand* (1) make a fight, (2) pass current (*royal*: 10-shilling piece)

POINS Sir John, I prithee, leave the prince and me alone.
I will lay him down such reasons for this adventure that
he shall go.

FALSTAFF Well, God give thee the spirit of persuasion
and him the ears of profiting, that what thou speakest
may move and what he hears may be believed, that the
true prince may (for recreation sake) prove a false thief;
146   for the poor abuses of the time want countenance. Farewell; you shall find me in Eastcheap.

148 PRINCE Farewell, thou latter spring! farewell, All-
hallown summer!   [Exit Falstaff.]

POINS Now, my good sweet honey lord, ride with us to-
morrow. I have a jest to execute that I cannot manage
alone. Falstaff, Bardolph, Peto, and Gadshill shall rob
153   those men that we have already waylaid; yourself and I
will not be there; and when they have the booty, if you
and I do not rob them, cut this head off from my
shoulders.

PRINCE How shall we part with them in setting forth?

POINS Why, we will set forth before or after them and ap-
point them a place of meeting, wherein it is at our
pleasure to fail; and then will they adventure upon the
exploit themselves, which they shall have no sooner
achieved, but we'll set upon them.

PRINCE Yea, but 'tis like that they will know us by our
164   horses, by our habits, and by every other appointment,
to be ourselves.

POINS Tut! our horses they shall not see – I'll tie them in
the wood; our vizards we will change after we leave
168   them; and, sirrah, I have cases of buckram for the
169   nonce, to immask our noted outward garments.

170 PRINCE Yea, but I doubt they will be too hard for us.

---

146 *countenance* encouragement   148–49 *All-hallown summer* Indian summer   153 *waylaid* set an ambush for   164 *appointment* accoutrement   168
sirrah sir (as a rule addressed to inferiors; here it implies familiarity); *cases*
suits   168–69 *for the nonce* for this purpose   169 *noted* well-known   170
doubt fear; *too hard* too much

POINS Well, for two of them, I know them to be as true-
bred cowards as ever turned back; and for the third, if
he fight longer than he sees reason, I'll forswear arms.
The virtue of this jest will be the incomprehensible lies 174
that this same fat rogue will tell us when we meet at
supper: how thirty, at least, he fought with; what wards, 176
what blows, what extremities he endured; and in the re- 177
proof of this lives the jest.

PRINCE Well, I'll go with thee. Provide us all things
necessary and meet me to-morrow night in Eastcheap.
There I'll sup. Farewell.

POINS Farewell, my lord.   *Exit.*

PRINCE
I know you all, and will awhile uphold
The unyoked humor of your idleness.   184
Yet herein will I imitate the sun,
Who doth permit the base contagious clouds   186
To smother up his beauty from the world,
That, when he please again to be himself,   188
Being wanted, he may be more wond'red at
By breaking through the foul and ugly mists
Of vapors that did seem to strangle him.
If all the year were playing holidays,
To sport would be as tedious as to work;
But when they seldom come, they wished-for come,
And nothing pleaseth but rare accidents.   195
So, when this loose behavior I throw off
And pay the debt I never promisèd,
By how much better than my word I am,
By so much shall I falsify men's hopes;   199
And, like bright metal on a sullen ground,
My reformation, glitt'ring o'er my fault,
Shall show more goodly and attract more eyes

174 *incomprehensible* unlimited 176 *wards* parries 177 *extremities* extreme
hazards; *reproof* disproof 184 *idleness* frivolity 186 *contagious* noxious
188 *That* so that 195 *accidents* events 199 *hopes* expectations

203 Than that which hath no foil to set it off.
204 I'll so offend to make offense a skill,
205 Redeeming time when men think least I will.   *Exit.*

*

I, iii   *Enter the King, Northumberland, Worcester,*
               Hotspur, Sir Walter Blunt, with others.

KING
My blood hath been too cold and temperate,
Unapt to stir at these indignities,
3   And you have found me, for accordingly
You tread upon my patience; but be sure
5   I will from henceforth rather be myself,
6   Mighty and to be feared, than my condition,
Which hath been smooth as oil, soft as young down,
And therefore lost that title of respect
Which the proud soul ne'er pays but to the proud.

WORCESTER
Our house, my sovereign liege, little deserves
The scourge of greatness to be used on it –
And that same greatness too which our own hands
13 Have holp to make so portly.

NORTHUMBERLAND
My lord –

KING
Worcester, get thee gone, for I do see
16 Danger and disobedience in thine eye.
O, sir, your presence is too bold and peremptory,
And majesty might never yet endure
19 The moody frontier of a servant brow.

---

203 *foil* contrast   204 *to* as to; *skill* piece of good policy   205 *Redeeming time* saving time from being lost
I, iii The Court of King Henry IV   3 *found me* found me out   5 *myself* i.e. every inch a king   6 *condition* (mild) natural disposition   13 *holp* helped; *portly* majestic   16 *Danger* defiance   19 *frontier* (literally) earthworks (alluding to 'front': forehead)

You have good leave to leave us: when we need
Your use and counsel, we shall send for you.
                              Exit Worcester.
You were about to speak.
NORTHUMBERLAND   Yea, my good lord.
Those prisoners in your highness' name demanded
Which Harry Percy here at Holmedon took,
Were, as he says, not with such strength denied
As is deliverèd to your majesty.   26
Either envy, therefore, or misprision   27
Is guilty of this fault, and not my son.

HOTSPUR
My liege, I did deny no prisoners.
But I remember, when the fight was done,
When I was dry with rage and extreme toil,
Breathless and faint, leaning upon my sword,
Came there a certain lord, neat and trimly dressed,
Fresh as a bridegroom, and his chin new reaped
Showed like a stubble land at harvest home.
He was perfumèd like a milliner,   36
And 'twixt his finger and his thumb he held
A pouncet box, which ever and anon   38
He gave his nose, and took't away again;
Who therewith angry, when it next came there,   40
Took it in snuff; and still he smiled and talked;   41
And as the soldiers bore dead bodies by,
He called them untaught knaves, unmannerly,
To bring a slovenly unhandsome corse   44
Betwixt the wind and his nobility.
With many holiday and lady terms   46
He questioned me, amongst the rest demanded   47

26 *deliverèd* reported   27 *envy* ill will; *misprision* misunderstanding   36
milliner (who sells scented gloves and other haberdashery)   38 *pouncet box*
perfume-box; *ever and anon* now and then   40 *Who* i.e. his nose   41 *Took
. . . snuff* (1) inhaled it, (2) resented (its being taken away); *still* continually
44 *slovenly* nasty   46 *holiday and lady* affected and effeminate   47 *questioned* kept on talking to

My prisoners in your majesty's behalf.
I then, all smarting with my wounds being cold,
To be so pestered with a popingay,

51 Out of my grief and my impatience
Answered neglectingly, I know not what –
He should, or he should not; for he made me mad
To see him shine so brisk, and smell so sweet,
And talk so like a waiting gentlewoman

56 Of guns and drums and wounds – God save the mark! –
57 And telling me the sovereignest thing on earth
58 Was parmacity for an inward bruise,
And that it was great pity, so it was,
This villainous saltpetre should be digged
Out of the bowels of the harmless earth,

62 Which many a good tall fellow had destroyed
So cowardly, and but for these vile guns,
He would himself have been a soldier.

65 This bald unjointed chat of his, my lord,
66 I answered indirectly, as I said,
And I beseech you, let not his report

68 Come current for an accusation
Betwixt my love and your high majesty.

BLUNT

The circumstance considered, good my lord,
Whate'er Lord Harry Percy then had said
To such a person, and in such a place,
At such a time, with all the rest retold,
May reasonably die, and never rise

75 To do him wrong, or any way impeach
What then he said, so he unsay it now.

KING

Why, yet he doth deny his prisoners,
But with proviso and exception,

---

51 *grief* pain (from wounds)   **56** *save the mark* avert anything so ridiculous **57** *sovereignest* most powerful (to cure)   **58** *parmacity* spermaceti ointment **62** *tall* stout   **65** *bald* trivial   **66** *indirectly* offhand   **68** *Come current* be accepted   **75** *do him wrong* put him in the wrong; *impeach* discredit

That we at our own charge shall ransom straight   79
His brother-in-law, the foolish Mortimer;
Who, on my soul, hath willfully betrayed
The lives of those that he did lead to fight
Against that great magician, damned Glendower,
Whose daughter, as we hear, that Earl of March
Hath lately married. Shall our coffers, then,
Be emptied to redeem a traitor home?
Shall we buy treason? and indent with fears   87
When they have lost and forfeited themselves?
No, on the barren mountains let him starve!
For I shall never hold that man my friend
Whose tongue shall ask me for one penny cost
To ransom home revolted Mortimer.

HOTSPUR
Revolted Mortimer?
He never did fall off, my sovereign liege,   94
But by the chance of war. To prove that true
Needs no more but one tongue for all those wounds,
Those mouthèd wounds, which valiantly he took   97
When on the gentle Severn's sedgy bank,
In single opposition hand to hand,
He did confound the best part of an hour   100
In changing hardiment with great Glendower.   101
Three times they breathed, and three times did they   102
   drink,
Upon agreement, of swift Severn's flood;
Who then, affrighted with their bloody looks,
Ran fearfully among the trembling reeds
And hid his crisp head in the hollow bank,   106
Bloodstainèd with these valiant combatants.
Never did bare and rotten policy   108
Color her working with such deadly wounds;   109

---

79 *straight* at once 87 *indent* make terms; *fears* what we fear 94 *fall off*
break his allegiance 97 *mouthèd* gaping 100 *confound* spend 101 *changing hardiment* trading blows 102 *breathed* stopped to catch their breath
106 *crisp* curly 108 *policy* craft 109 *Color* disguise

Nor never could the noble Mortimer
Receive so many, and all willingly.
Then let not him be slandered with revolt.

KING

113   Thou dost belie him, Percy, thou dost belie him!
He never did encounter with Glendower.
I tell thee
He durst as well have met the devil alone
As Owen Glendower for an enemy.
Art thou not ashamed? But, sirrah, henceforth
Let me not hear you speak of Mortimer.
Send me your prisoners with the speediest means,
Or you shall hear in such a kind from me
As will displease you. My Lord Northumberland,
We license your departure with your son. –
Send us your prisoners, or you will hear of it.
                    Exeunt King [, Blunt, and train].

HOTSPUR

An if the devil come and roar for them,
126   I will not send them. I will after straight
And tell him so; for I will ease my heart,
Albeit I make a hazard of my head.

NORTHUMBERLAND

129   What, drunk with choler? Stay, and pause awhile.
Here comes your uncle.
      Enter Worcester.

HOTSPUR   Speak of Mortimer?
Zounds, I will speak of him, and let my soul
Want mercy if I do not join with him!
Yea, on his part I'll empty all these veins,
And shed my dear blood drop by drop in the dust,
But I will lift the downtrod Mortimer
As high in the air as this unthankful king,
137   As this ingrate and cankered Bolingbroke.

---

113 *belie* tell lies about   126 *will after* will go after   129 *choler* anger   137
cankered corrupt

NORTHUMBERLAND
Brother, the king hath made your nephew mad.

WORCESTER
Who struck this heat up after I was gone?

HOTSPUR
He will (forsooth) have all my prisoners;   140
And when I urged the ransom once again
Of my wive's brother, then his cheek looked pale,
And on my face he turned an eye of death,   143
Trembling even at the name of Mortimer.

WORCESTER
I cannot blame him. Was not he proclaimed
By Richard that dead is, the next of blood?

NORTHUMBERLAND
He was; I heard the proclamation.
And then it was when the unhappy king
(Whose wrongs in us God pardon!) did set forth   149
Upon his Irish expedition;
From whence he intercepted did return
To be deposed, and shortly murderèd.

WORCESTER
And for whose death we in the world's wide mouth
Live scandalized and foully spoken of.

HOTSPUR
But soft, I pray you. Did King Richard then   155
Proclaim my brother Edmund Mortimer   156
Heir to the crown?

NORTHUMBERLAND He did; myself did hear it.

HOTSPUR
Nay, then I cannot blame his cousin king,
That wished him on the barren mountains starve.
But shall it be that you, that set the crown
Upon the head of this forgetful man,
And for his sake wear the detested blot

---

140 *forsooth* indeed, in truth   143 *death* deadly fear   149 *wrongs in us* wrongs suffered because of us   155 *soft* hold on, wait a minute   156 *brother* i.e. brother-in-law

163   Of murderous subornation – shall it be
That you a world of curses undergo,
Being the agents or base second means,
The cords, the ladder, or the hangman rather?
O, pardon me that I descend so low

168   To show the line and the predicament
Wherein you range under this subtle king!
Shall it for shame be spoken in these days,
Or fill up chronicles in time to come,
That men of your nobility and power

173   Did gage them both in an unjust behalf
(As both of you, God pardon it! have done)
To put down Richard, that sweet lovely rose,

176   And plant this thorn, this canker, Bolingbroke?
And shall it in more shame be further spoken
That you are fooled, discarded, and shook off
By him for whom these shames ye underwent?
No! yet time serves wherein you may redeem

181   Your banished honors and restore yourselves
Into the good thoughts of the world again;

183   Revenge the jeering and disdained contempt
Of this proud king, who studies day and night

185   To answer all the debt he owes to you
Even with the bloody payment of your deaths.
Therefore I say –

187 WORCESTER   Peace, cousin, say no more;
And now I will unclasp a secret book,

189   And to your quick-conceiving discontents
I'll read you matter deep and dangerous,
As full of peril and adventurous spirit
As to o'erwalk a current roaring loud
On the unsteadfast footing of a spear.

---

163 *murderous subornation* prompting of murder   168 *line* station; *predicament* category   173 *gage* bind; *in . . . behalf* for the benefit of injustice   176 *canker* (1) wild rose, (2) ulcer   181 *banished* forfeited   183 *disdained* disdainful   185 *answer* satisfy   187 *Peace* be quiet, hold your tongue   189 *quick-conceiving* understanding quickly

HOTSPUR

If he fall in, good night, or sink or swim!   194
Send danger from the east unto the west,
So honor cross it from the north to south,   196
And let them grapple. O, the blood more stirs
To rouse a lion than to start a hare!

NORTHUMBERLAND

Imagination of some great exploit
Drives him beyond the bounds of patience.   200

HOTSPUR

By heaven, methinks it were an easy leap
To pluck bright honor from the pale-faced moon,
Or dive into the bottom of the deep,
Where fathom line could never touch the ground,
And pluck up drownèd honor by the locks,
So he that doth redeem her thence might wear   206
Without corrival all her dignities;   207
But out upon this half-faced fellowship!   208

WORCESTER

He apprehends a world of figures here,   209
But not the form of what he should attend.   210
Good cousin, give me audience for a while.

HOTSPUR

I cry you mercy.   212

WORCESTER   Those same noble Scots
That are your prisoners—

HOTSPUR   I'll keep them all.
By God, he shall not have a Scot of them!
No, if a Scot would save his soul, he shall not.
I'll keep them, by this hand!

WORCESTER   You start away
And lend no ear unto my purposes.

---

194 *he* i.e. the man on the spear; *or . . . swim* whether he sinks or swims   196
So so that   200 *patience* self-control   206 *So* provided that   207 *corrival*
partner   208 *out upon* away with; *half-faced fellowship* sharing honor fifty-
fifty   209 *figures* figments of the imagination   210 *form* essence; *attend* give
his attention to   212 *cry you mercy* beg your pardon

Those prisoners you shall keep.

HOTSPUR   Nay, I will! That's flat!
He said he would not ransom Mortimer,
Forbade my tongue to speak of Mortimer,
But I will find him when he lies asleep,
And in his ear I'll hollo 'Mortimer.'
Nay, I'll have a starling shall be taught to speak
Nothing but 'Mortimer,' and give it him
225 To keep his anger still in motion.

WORCESTER
Hear you, cousin, a word.

HOTSPUR
227 All studies here I solemnly defy
Save how to gall and pinch this Bolingbroke;
229 And that same sword-and-buckler Prince of Wales:
But that I think his father loves him not
And would be glad he met with some mischance,
I would have him poisoned with a pot of ale.

WORCESTER
Farewell, kinsman. I will talk to you
When you are better tempered to attend.

NORTHUMBERLAND
Why, what a wasp-stung and impatient fool
Art thou to break into this woman's mood,
Tying thine ear to no tongue but thine own!

HOTSPUR
Why, look you, I am whipped and scourged with rods,
239 Nettled, and stung with pismires when I hear
240 Of this vile politician, Bolingbroke.
In Richard's time – what do you call the place?
A plague upon it! it is in Gloucestershire;
243 'Twas where the madcap duke his uncle kept,
244 His uncle York – where I first bowed my knee
Unto this king of smiles, this Bolingbroke –

---

225 *still* ever 227 *studies* interests; *defy* renounce 229 *sword-and-buckler* ruffianly 239 *pismires* ants 240 *politician* ignoble schemer 243 *kept* dwelt 244 *bowed* (see *Richard II*, II, iii)

'Sblood! – when you and he came back from Ravenspurgh –

NORTHUMBERLAND
  At Berkeley Castle.

HOTSPUR
  You say true.
  Why, what a candy deal of courtesy   249
  This fawning greyhound then did proffer me!
  'Look when his infant fortune came to age,'
  And 'gentle Harry Percy,' and 'kind cousin' –   252
  O, the devil take such cozeners! – God forgive me!   253
  Good uncle, tell your tale, for I have done.

WORCESTER
  Nay, if you have not, to it again.
  We will stay your leisure.   256

HOTSPUR   I have done, i' faith.

WORCESTER
  Then once more to your Scottish prisoners.
  Deliver them up without their ransom straight,
  And make the Douglas' son your only mean
  For powers in Scotland – which, for divers reasons
  Which I shall send you written, be assured
  Will easily be granted.
            [To Northumberland] You, my lord,
  Your son in Scotland being thus employed,
  Shall secretly into the bosom creep
  Of that same noble prelate well-beloved,
  The archbishop.

HOTSPUR   Of York, is it not?

WORCESTER
  True; who bears hard   267
  His brother's death at Bristow, the Lord Scroop.   268
  I speak not this in estimation,   269
  As what I think might be, but what I know

249 *candy* sugary   252 *gentle* of gentle birth   253 *cozeners* cheaters   256
stay await   267 *bears hard* resents   268 *Scroop* Earl of Wiltshire (*Richard
II*, III, ii)   269 *in estimation* conjecturally

Is ruminated, plotted, and set down,
And only stays but to behold the face
Of that occasion that shall bring it on.

HOTSPUR
I smell it. Upon my life, it will do well.

NORTHUMBERLAND
275   Before the game is afoot thou still let'st slip.

HOTSPUR
Why, it cannot choose but be a noble plot.
And then the power of Scotland and of York
To join with Mortimer, ha?

WORCESTER   And so they shall.

HOTSPUR
In faith, it is exceedingly well aimed.

WORCESTER
And 'tis no little reason bids us speed
281   To save our heads by raising of a head;
282   For, bear ourselves as even as we can,
The king will always think him in our debt,
And think we think ourselves unsatisfied,
285   Till he hath found a time to pay us home.
And see already how he doth begin
To make us strangers to his looks of love.

HOTSPUR
He does, he does! We'll be revenged on him.

WORCESTER
Cousin, farewell. No further go in this
Than I by letters shall direct your course.
291   When time is ripe, which will be suddenly,
I'll steal to Glendower and Lord Mortimer,
Where you and Douglas, and our pow'rs at once,
As I will fashion it, shall happily meet,
To bear our fortunes in our own strong arms,
Which now we hold at much uncertainty.

---

275 *still* always; *slip* loose the dogs   281 *head* army   282 *even* carefully
285 *home* fully   291 *suddenly* at once

NORTHUMBERLAND
Farewell, good brother. We shall thrive, I trust.
HOTSPUR
Uncle, adieu. O, let the hours be short
Till fields and blows and groans applaud our sport!
Exeunt.

*

Enter a Carrier with a lantern in his hand.   II, i
1. CARRIER Heigh-ho! an it be not four by the day, I'll be   1
hanged. Charles' wain is over the new chimney, and yet   2
our horse not packed. – What, ostler!   3
OSTLER *[within]* Anon, anon.   4
1. CARRIER I prithee, Tom, beat Cut's saddle, put a few
flocks in the point. Poor jade is wrung in the withers out   6
of all cess.
Enter another Carrier.
2. CARRIER Peas and beans are as dank here as a dog, and   8
that is the next way to give poor jades the bots. This   9
house is turned upside down since Robin Ostler died.
1. CARRIER Poor fellow never joyed since the price of oats
rose. It was the death of him.
2. CARRIER I think this be the most villainous house in all
London road for fleas. I am stung like a tench.   14
1. CARRIER Like a tench? By the mass, there is ne'er a
king christen could be better bit than I have been since   16
the first cock.   17
2. CARRIER Why, they will allow us ne'er a jordan, and   18

II, i An inn yard at Rochester   1 *four . . . day* four in the morning   2
Charles' wain the Great Bear   3 *horse* horses   4 *Anon* right away   6 *flocks*
tufts of wool; *point* pommel; *jade* (contemptuous name for) horse; *wrung*
chafed   6–7 *out . . . cess* beyond estimation   8 *Peas and beans* fodder for
horses; *as dank . . . dog* i.e. very soggy   9 *next* quickest; *bots* maggots in
the intestines   14 *tench* a fish whose red spots may be likened to flea-bites
16 *king christen* Christian king   17 *first cock* i.e. midnight   18 *jordan*
chamberpot

19   then we leak in your chimney, and your chamber-lye
20   breeds fleas like a loach.

21 1. CARRIER What, ostler! come away and be hanged!
    come away!

23 2. CARRIER I have a gammon of bacon and two razes of
    ginger, to be delivered as far as Charing Cross.

    1. CARRIER God's body! the turkeys in my pannier are
    quite starved. What, ostler! A plague on thee! hast thou
    never an eye in thy head? Canst not hear? An 'twere not
28   as good deed as drink to break the pate on thee, I am a
29   very villain. Come, and be hanged! Hast no faith in
    thee?

       Enter Gadshill.

GADSHILL Good morrow, carriers. What's o'clock?

1. CARRIER I think it be two o'clock.

GADSHILL I prithee lend me thy lantern to see my gelding in the stable.

1. CARRIER Nay, by God, soft! I know a trick worth two
of that, i' faith.

GADSHILL I pray thee lend me thine.

37 2. CARRIER Ay, when? canst tell? Lend me thy lantern,
    quoth he? Marry, I'll see thee hanged first!

GADSHILL Sirrah carrier, what time do you mean to
come to London?

2. CARRIER Time enough to go to bed with a candle, I
warrant thee. Come, neighbor Mugs, we'll call up the
43   gentlemen. They will along with company, for they
44   have great charge.   *Exeunt [Carriers].*

45 GADSHILL What, ho! chamberlain!

       Enter Chamberlain.

46 CHAMBERLAIN At hand, quoth pickpurse.

---

19 *chimney* fireplace; *chamber-lye* urine   20 *like a loach* as a loach (a prolific
fish) breeds loaches   21 *come away* come here   23 *gammon of bacon* ham;
razes roots   28 *the pate on thee* your head   29 *faith* trustworthiness   37 *Ay*
. . . *tell* i.e. never   43 *will along* wish to go along   44 *charge* baggage   45
chamberlain male servant corresponding to chambermaid   46 *At . . . pickpurse* (proverbial)

GADSHILL That's even as fair as 'at hand, quoth the 47
chamberlain'; for thou variest no more from picking of
purses than giving direction doth from laboring: thou
layest the plot how.

CHAMBERLAIN Good morrow, Master Gadshill. It holds 51
current that I told you yesternight. There's a franklin in 52
the Wild of Kent hath brought three hundred marks 53
with him in gold. I heard him tell it to one of his company last night at supper – a kind of auditor, one that
hath abundance of charge too, God knows what. They
are up already and call for eggs and butter. They will
away presently.   58

GADSHILL Sirrah, if they meet not with Saint Nicholas' 59
clerks, I'll give thee this neck.

CHAMBERLAIN No, I'll none of it. I pray thee keep that 61
for the hangman; for I know thou worshippest Saint
Nicholas as truly as a man of falsehood may.

GADSHILL What talkest thou to me of the hangman? If I
hang, I'll make a fat pair of gallows; for if I hang, old Sir
John hangs with me, and thou knowest he is no starveling. Tut! there are other Troyans that thou dream'st 67
not of, the which for sport sake are content to do the
profession some grace; that would (if matters should be 69
looked into) for their own credit sake make all whole. I
am joined with no foot land-rakers, no long-staff six- 71
penny strikers, none of these mad mustachio purple- 72
hued maltworms; but with nobility and tranquillity, 73
burgomasters and great oneyers, such as can hold in, 74
such as will strike sooner than speak, and speak sooner 75

---

47 *fair* apt   51–52 *holds current* is still true   52 *franklin* small landowner
53 *Wild* forest; *three hundred marks* £200   58 *presently* at once   59–60
Saint Nicholas' clerks highwaymen   61 *I'll none* I want none   67 *Troyans*
sports   69 *profession* i.e. robbery; *grace* credit   71 *foot land-rakers* footpads
72 *strikers* holdup men   72–73 *mustachio . . . maltworms* topers with mus-
taches stained with beer   73 *tranquillity* those who live an easy life   74
oneyers officers; *hold in* keep their mouths shut   75 *speak* i.e. say 'hands up'

than drink, and drink sooner than pray; and yet, zounds, I lie; for they pray continually to their saint, the commonwealth, or rather, not pray to her, but prey on her, for they ride up and down on her and make her
79   their boots.

   CHAMBERLAIN What, the commonwealth their boots?
81   Will she hold out water in foul way?
82 GADSHILL She will, she will! Justice hath liquored her.
83   We steal as in a castle, cocksure. We have the receipt of
84   fernseed, we walk invisible.

   CHAMBERLAIN Nay, by my faith, I think you are more beholding to the night than to fernseed for your walking invisible.

   GADSHILL Give me thy hand. Thou shalt have a share in
89   our purchase, as I am a true man.

   CHAMBERLAIN Nay, rather let me have it, as you are a false thief.

92 GADSHILL Go to; 'homo' is a common name to all men. Bid the ostler bring my gelding out of the stable.
94   Farewell, you muddy knave.   *[Exeunt.]*

*

II, ii   *Enter Prince, Poins, Peto [and Bardolph].*
   POINS Come, shelter, shelter! I have removed Falstaff's
2   horse, and he frets like a gummed velvet.
3 PRINCE Stand close.   *[They step aside.]*
     Enter Falstaff.
   FALSTAFF Poins! Poins, and be hanged! Poins!
5 PRINCE *[comes forward]* Peace, ye fat-kidneyed rascal!

---

79 *boots* booty   81 *foul way* muddy road, i.e. tight place   82 *liquored* (1) greased, (2) bribed   83 *as ... castle* with impunity   84 *fernseed* reputed to be invisible and to confer invisibility   89 *purchase* loot; *true* honest   92 *Go to* 'nuts'; '*homo*' ... *men* i.e. they're all the same   94 *muddy* stupid
II, ii The highway at Gad's Hill   2 *frets* (1) fumes, (2) wears away; *gummed velvet* velvet stiffened with gum (and therefore liable to wear)   3 *close* where you won't be seen   5 *rascal* (literally) lean deer

What a brawling dost thou keep!   6

FALSTAFF Where's Poins, Hal?

PRINCE He is walked up to the top of the hill; I'll go seek him.   *[Steps aside.]*

FALSTAFF I am accursed to rob in that thieve's company. The rascal hath removed my horse and tied him I know not where. If I travel but four foot by the squire further 12 afoot, I shall break my wind. Well, I doubt not but to die a fair death for all this, if I scape hanging for killing that rogue. I have forsworn his company hourly any time this two-and-twenty years, and yet I am bewitched with the rogue's company. If the rascal have not given me medicines to make me love him, I'll be hanged. It 18 could not be else: I have drunk medicines. Poins! Hal! A plague upon you both! Bardolph! Peto! I'll starve ere I'll rob a foot further. An 'twere not as good a deed as drink to turn true man and to leave these rogues, I am 22 the veriest varlet that ever chewed with a tooth. Eight 23 yards of uneven ground is threescore and ten miles afoot with me, and the stony-hearted villains know it well enough. A plague upon it when thieves cannot be true one to another! *(They whistle.)* Whew! A plague upon you all! Give me my horse, you rogues! give me my horse and be hanged!

PRINCE *[comes forward]* Peace, ye fat-guts! Lie down, lay thine ear close to the ground, and list if thou canst hear the tread of travellers.

FALSTAFF Have you any levers to lift me up again, being down? 'Sblood, I'll not bear mine own flesh so far afoot again for all the coin in thy father's exchequer. What a plague mean ye to colt me thus?   35

PRINCE Thou liest; thou art not colted, thou art un-colted.

FALSTAFF I prithee, good Prince Hal, help me to my

---

6 *keep* keep up   12 *squire* foot-rule   18 *medicines* love potions   22 *true* honest   23 *varlet* scamp   35 *colt* befool

horse, good king's son.

39 PRINCE Out, ye rogue! Shall I be your ostler?

FALSTAFF Go hang thyself in thine own heir-apparent
41   garters! If I be ta'en, I'll peach for this. An I have not
42   ballads made on you all, and sung to filthy tunes, let a
cup of sack be my poison. When a jest is so forward –
and afoot too – I hate it.
Enter Gadshill.

GADSHILL Stand!

FALSTAFF So I do, against my will.

47 POINS *[comes forward]* O, 'tis our setter; I know his voice.

BARDOLPH What news?

49 GADSHILL Case ye, case ye! On with your vizards!
There's money of the king's coming down the hill; 'tis
going to the king's exchequer.

FALSTAFF You lie, ye rogue! 'Tis going to the king's
tavern.

53 GADSHILL There's enough to make us all.

FALSTAFF To be hanged.

PRINCE Sirs, you four shall front them in the narrow
lane; Ned Poins and I will walk lower. If they scape
from your encounter, then they light on us.

PETO How many be there of them?

GADSHILL Some eight or ten.

FALSTAFF Zounds, will they not rob us?

PRINCE What, a coward, Sir John Paunch?

FALSTAFF Indeed, I am not John of Gaunt, your grandfather, but yet no coward, Hal.

64 PRINCE Well, we leave that to the proof.

POINS Sirrah Jack, thy horse stands behind the hedge.
When thou need'st him, there thou shalt find him. Farewell and stand fast.

FALSTAFF Now cannot I strike him, if I should be hanged.

---

39 *Out* get out 41 *ta'en* arrested 42 *ballads* (scurrilous) songs 47 *setter*
one who sets a match (I, ii, 100) 49 *Case ye* put on your masks 53 *make us
all* make our fortunes 64 *proof* test

PRINCE *[aside to Poins]* Ned, where are our disguises?

POINS *[aside to Prince]* Here, hard by. Stand close.

[Exeunt Prince and Poins.]

FALSTAFF Now, my masters, happy man be his dole, say 71
I. Every man to his business.

Enter the Travellers.

TRAVELLER Come, neighbor. The boy shall lead our
horses down the hill; we'll walk afoot awhile and ease
our legs.

THIEVES Stand!

TRAVELLER Jesus bless us!

FALSTAFF Strike! down with them! cut the villains'
throats! Ah, whoreson caterpillars! bacon-fed knaves! 78
they hate us youth. Down with them! fleece them!

TRAVELLER O, we are undone, both we and ours for ever! 80

FALSTAFF Hang ye, gorbellied knaves, are ye undone? 81
No, ye fat chuffs; I would your store were here! On, 82
bacons, on! What, ye knaves! young men must live. 83
You are grandjurors, are ye? We'll jure ye, faith! 84

Here they rob them and bind them. Exeunt.

Enter the Prince and Poins [in buckram suits].

PRINCE The thieves have bound the true men. Now 85
could thou and I rob the thieves and go merrily to
London, it would be argument for a week, laughter for a 87
month, and a good jest for ever.

POINS Stand close! I hear them coming.

[They stand aside.]

Enter the Thieves again.

FALSTAFF Come, my masters, let us share, and then to
horse before day. An the prince and Poins be not two
arrant cowards, there's no equity stirring. There's no 92
more valor in that Poins than in a wild duck. 93

---

71 *dole* lot 78 *caterpillars* parasites 80 *ours* our families 81 *gorbellied* fat-
paunched 82 *chuffs* misers; *your store* all your possessions 83 *bacons* fat
men 84 *grandjurors* i.e. well-to-do citizens 85 *true* honest 87 *argument*
something to talk about 92 *arrant* out-and-out; *equity* judicial discern-
ment 93 *wild duck* notoriously timid

PRINCE
Your money!

POINS
Villains!

⎰ *As they are sharing, the prince and Poins*
⎱ *set upon them. They all run away, and*
⎰ *Falstaff, after a blow or two, runs away*
⎱ *too, leaving the booty behind them.*

PRINCE Got with much ease. Now merrily to horse. The thieves are all scattered, and possessed with fear so strongly that they dare not meet each other: each takes his fellow for an officer. Away, good Ned. Falstaff sweats to death and lards the lean earth as he walks along. Were't not for laughing, I should pity him.

POINS How the fat rogue roared!   *Exeunt.*

*

II, iii   *Enter Hotspur solus, reading a letter.*

HOTSPUR 'But, for mine own part, my lord, I could be
2   well contented to be there, in respect of the love I bear
3   your house.' He could be contented – why is he not then? In respect of the love he bears our house! He shows in this he loves his own barn better than he loves our house. Let me see some more. 'The purpose you undertake is dangerous' – why, that's certain! 'Tis dangerous to take a cold, to sleep, to drink; but I tell you, my lord fool, out of this nettle, danger, we pluck this flower, safety. 'The purpose you undertake is dangerous, the friends you have named uncertain, the
12   time itself unsorted, and your whole plot too light for the counterpoise of so great an opposition.' Say you so, say you so? I say unto you again, you are a shallow,
14   cowardly hind, and you lie. What a lackbrain is this! By the Lord, our plot is a good plot as ever was laid; our friends true and constant: a good plot, good friends, and
17   full of expectation; an excellent plot, very good friends.

II, iii Hotspur's castle (at Warkworth)   **2** *in respect of* on account of   **3**
house family   **12** *unsorted* ill-chosen   **12-13** *for the counterpoise of* to counterbalance   **14** *hind* peasant   **17** *expectation* promise

What a frosty-spirited rogue is this! Why, my Lord of
York commends the plot and the general course of the
action. Zounds, an I were now by this rascal, I could
brain him with his lady's fan. Is there not my father, my
uncle, and myself; Lord Edmund Mortimer, my Lord
of York, and Owen Glendower? Is there not, besides,
the Douglas? Have I not all their letters to meet me in
arms by the ninth of the next month, and are they not
some of them set forward already? What a pagan rascal   26
is this! an infidel! Ha! you shall see now, in very sin-   27
cerity of fear and cold heart will he to the king and lay
open all our proceedings. O, I could divide myself and
go to buffets for moving such a dish of skim milk with so   30
honorable an action! Hang him, let him tell the king!
we are prepared. I will set forward to-night.
     Enter his Lady.
How now, Kate? I must leave you within these two
hours.

LADY

O my good lord, why are you thus alone?
For what offense have I this fortnight been
A banished woman from my Harry's bed?
Tell me, sweet lord, what is't that takes from thee
Thy stomach, pleasure, and thy golden sleep?   38
Why dost thou bend thine eyes upon the earth,
And start so often when thou sit'st alone?
Why hast thou lost the fresh blood in thy cheeks
And given my treasures and my rights of thee
To thick-eyed musing and cursed melancholy?   43
In thy faint slumbers I by thee have watched,
And heard thee murmur tales of iron wars,
Speak terms of manage to thy bounding steed,   46
Cry 'Courage! to the field!' And thou hast talked

---

26 *pagan* unbelieving 27 *very* veritable 30 *go to buffets* fall to blows 38
stomach appetite 43 *thick-eyed* dim-sighted 46 *manage* horsemanship

Of sallies and retires, of trenches, tents,
49 Of palisadoes, frontiers, parapets,
50 Of basilisks, of cannon, culverin,
Of prisoners' ransom, and of soldiers slain,
52 And all the currents of a heady fight.
Thy spirit within thee hath been so at war,
And thus hath so bestirred thee in thy sleep,
That beads of sweat have stood upon thy brow
Like bubbles in a late-disturbèd stream,
And in thy face strange motions have appeared,
Such as we see when men restrain their breath
59 On some great sudden hest. O, what portents are these?
60 Some heavy business hath my lord in hand,
And I must know it, else he loves me not.

HOTSPUR
What, ho!
[Enter a Servant.]
                    Is Gilliams with the packet gone?
SERVANT
He is, my lord, an hour ago.
HOTSPUR
Hath Butler brought those horses from the sheriff?
SERVANT
One horse, my lord, he brought even now.
HOTSPUR
What horse? A roan, a crop-ear, is it not?
SERVANT
It is, my lord.
HOTSPUR   That roan shall be my throne.
68 Well, I will back him straight. O esperancè!
Bid Butler lead him forth into the park.   *[Exit Servant.]*
LADY
But hear you, my lord.

49 *palisadoes* stakes set in the ground to stop a charge; *frontiers* outworks
50 *basilisks, culverin* kinds of cannon   52 *heady* headlong   59 *hest* command, i.e. when making a special effort   60 *heavy* (1) weighty, (2) woeful
68 *esperancè* hope (the Percy battle-cry)

HOTSPUR
What say'st thou, my lady?

LADY
What is it carries you away?

HOTSPUR
Why, my horse, my love – my horse!

LADY
Out, you mad-headed ape!
A weasel hath not such a deal of spleen   75
As you are tossed with. In faith,
I'll know your business, Harry; that I will!
I fear my brother Mortimer doth stir
About his title and hath sent for you   79
To line his enterprise; but if you go –   80

HOTSPUR
So far afoot, I shall be weary, love.

LADY
Come, come, you paraquito, answer me   82
Directly unto this question that I ask.
In faith, I'll break thy little finger, Harry,
An if thou wilt not tell me all things true.

HOTSPUR
Away, away, you trifler! Love? I love thee not;
I care not for thee, Kate. This is no world
To play with mammets and to tilt with lips.   88
We must have bloody noses and cracked crowns,
And pass them current too. Gods me, my horse!   90
What say'st thou, Kate? What wouldst thou have
    with me?

LADY
Do you not love me? do you not indeed?
Well, do not then; for since you love me not,
I will not love myself. Do you not love me?

---

75 *weasel* proverbially quarrelsome; *spleen* irascibility . . **79** *title* claim to the
throne   **80** *line* reinforce   **82** *paraquito* parrot   **88** *mammets* dolls   **90** *pass
them current* (1) deal them out, (2) circulate (*crowns*: 5-shilling pieces); *Gods
me* God save me

Nay, tell me if you speak in jest or no.

HOTSPUR

Come, wilt thou see me ride?
And when I am a-horseback, I will swear
I love thee infinitely. But hark you, Kate:
I must not have you henceforth question me
100   Whither I go, nor reason whereabout.
Whither I must, I must, and to conclude,
This evening must I leave you, gentle Kate.
I know you wise, but yet no farther wise
Than Harry Percy's wife; constant you are,
But yet a woman; and for secrecy,
No lady closer, for I well believe
Thou wilt not utter what thou dost not know,
And so far will I trust thee, gentle Kate.

LADY

How? so far?

HOTSPUR

Not an inch further. But hark you, Kate:
Whither I go, thither shall you go too;
To-day will I set forth, to-morrow you.
Will this content you, Kate?

113 LADY   It must of force.   *Exeunt.*

*

II, iv   *Enter Prince and Poins.*

1 PRINCE Ned, prithee come out of that fat room and lend
me thy hand to laugh a little.

POINS Where hast been, Hal?

4 PRINCE With three or four loggerheads amongst three or
fourscore hogsheads. I have sounded the very bass-
6   string of humility. Sirrah, I am sworn brother to a leash

---

100 *reason whereabout* discuss what for   113 *of force* of necessity
II, iv Within an Eastcheap tavern   1 *fat* stuffy   4 *loggerheads* blockheads
6 *leash* i.e. three

of drawers and can call them all by their christen names, 7
as Tom, Dick, and Francis. They take it already upon
their salvation that, though I be but Prince of Wales,
yet I am the king of courtesy, and tell me flatly I am no
proud Jack like Falstaff, but a Corinthian, a lad of 11
mettle, a good boy (by the Lord, so they call me!), and 12
when I am king of England I shall command all the
good lads in Eastcheap. They call drinking deep, dye-
ing scarlet; and when you breathe in your watering, 15
they cry 'hem!' and bid you play it off. To conclude, I 16
am so good a proficient in one quarter of an hour that I
can drink with any tinker in his own language during
my life. I tell thee, Ned, thou hast lost much honor that
thou wert not with me in this action. But, sweet Ned – 19
to sweeten which name of Ned, I give thee this pennyworth of sugar, clapped even now into my hand by an 21
under-skinker, one that never spake other English in his 22
life than 'Eight shillings and sixpence,' and 'You are
welcome,' with this shrill addition, 'Anon, anon, sir! 24
Score a pint of bastard in the Half-moon,' or so – but, 25
Ned, to drive away the time till Falstaff come, I prithee
do thou stand in some by-room while I question my
puny drawer to what end he gave me the sugar; and do
thou never leave calling 'Francis!' that his tale to me
may be nothing but 'Anon!' Step aside, and I'll show
thee a precedent. 31
POINS Francis!
PRINCE Thou art perfect. 33
POINS Francis!   *[Exit Poins.]*

---

7 *drawers* waiters   11 *Corinthian* good sport   12 *a good boy* one of the boys
15 *scarlet* the best scarlet dyes were made with topers' urine; *breathe* pause;
watering drinking   16 *play* i.e. toss   19 *action* encounter, (literally) battle
21 *sugar* used to sweeten wine   22 *under-skinker* bartender's assistant   24
Anon i.e. coming   25 *bastard* sweet Spanish wine; *Half-moon* a room in the
tavern   31 *precedent* something worth following   33 *Thou art perfect* you
have learned your part

Enter [Francis, a] Drawer.

35 FRANCIS Anon, anon, sir. – Look down into the Pomgarnet, Ralph.

PRINCE Come hither, Francis.

FRANCIS My lord?

39 PRINCE How long hast thou to serve, Francis?

FRANCIS Forsooth, five years, and as much as to –

POINS *[within]* Francis!

FRANCIS Anon, anon, sir.

PRINCE Five year! by'r Lady, a long lease for the clinking of pewter. But, Francis, darest thou be so valiant as to play the coward with thy indenture and show it a fair pair of heels and run from it?

47 FRANCIS O Lord, sir, I'll be sworn upon all the books in England I could find in my heart –

POINS *[within]* Francis!

FRANCIS Anon, sir.

PRINCE How old art thou, Francis?

52 FRANCIS Let me see: about Michaelmas next I shall be –

POINS *[within]* Francis!

FRANCIS Anon, sir. Pray stay a little, my lord.

PRINCE Nay, but hark you, Francis. For the sugar thou gavest me – 'twas a pennyworth, was't not?

FRANCIS O Lord! I would it had been two!

PRINCE I will give thee for it a thousand pound. Ask me when thou wilt, and thou shalt have it.

POINS *[within]* Francis!

FRANCIS Anon, anon.

PRINCE Anon, Francis? No, Francis; but to-morrow,
63 Francis; or, Francis, a Thursday; or indeed, Francis, when thou wilt. But, Francis –

FRANCIS My lord?

66 PRINCE Wilt thou rob this leathern-jerkin, crystal-

---

35 *Pomgarnet* Pomegranate (a room in the tavern)　39 *serve* i.e. as an apprentice　47 *books* i.e. Bibles　52 *Michaelmas* September 29　63 *a* on　66 *rob* i.e. by running away

button, not-pated, agate-ring, puke-stocking, caddis- 67
garter, smooth-tongue, Spanish-pouch –

FRANCIS O Lord, sir, who do you mean?

PRINCE Why then, your brown bastard is your only
drink; for look you, Francis, your white canvas doublet 71
will sully. In Barbary, sir, it cannot come to so much.   72

FRANCIS What, sir?

POINS *[within]* Francis!

PRINCE Away, you rogue! Dost thou not hear them
call?   76

> *Here they both call him. The Drawer stands amazed,*
> *not knowing which way to go.*
> *Enter Vintner.*

VINTNER What, stand'st thou still, and hear'st such a
calling? Look to the guests within. *[Exit Francis.]* My
lord, old Sir John, with half-a-dozen more, are at the
door. Shall I let them in?

PRINCE Let them alone awhile, and then open the door.
[Exit Vintner.] Poins!

POINS *[within]* Anon, anon, sir.

> *Enter Poins.*

PRINCE Sirrah, Falstaff and the rest of the thieves are at
the door. Shall we be merry?

POINS As merry as crickets, my lad. But hark ye; what
cunning match have you made with this jest of the 87
drawer? Come, what's the issue?   88

PRINCE I am now of all humors that have showed themselves humors since the old days of goodman Adam to
the pupil age of this present twelve o'clock at midnight.   91
[Enter Francis.]
What's o'clock, Francis?

FRANCIS Anon, anon, sir.   *[Exit.]*

---

67 *not-pated* short-haired; *agate-ring* seal ring; *puke-stocking* woolen-stock-
ing; *caddis-garter* garter of worsted tape   71–72 *your . . . sully* i.e. you'll
have to put up with a drawer's life   72 *it* i.e. sugar, imported from Barbary
76 s.d. *amazed* dumbfounded   87 *cunning match* sly game   88 *issue* outcome   91 *pupil age* youth

PRINCE That ever this fellow should have fewer words than a parrot, and yet the son of a woman! His industry
96 is upstairs and downstairs, his eloquence the parcel of a reckoning. I am not yet of Percy's mind, the Hotspur of
98 the North; he that kills me some six or seven dozen of Scots at a breakfast, washes his hands, and says to his wife, 'Fie upon this quiet life! I want work.' 'O my sweet Harry,' says she, 'how many hast thou killed to-
102 day?' 'Give my roan horse a drench,' says he, and answers 'Some fourteen,' an hour after, 'a trifle, a trifle.' I prithee call in Falstaff. I'll play Percy, and that
105 damned brawn shall play Dame Mortimer his wife.
106 'Rivo!' says the drunkard. Call in ribs, call in tallow.

Enter Falstaff [, Gadshill, Bardolph, and Peto ; Francis follows with wine].

POINS Welcome, Jack. Where hast thou been?
108 FALSTAFF A plague of all cowards, I say, and a vengeance too! Marry and amen! Give me a cup of sack,
110 boy. Ere I lead this life long, I'll sew netherstocks, and mend them and foot them too. A plague of all cowards!
112 Give me a cup of sack, rogue. Is there no virtue extant?
He drinketh.

113 PRINCE Didst thou never see Titan kiss a dish of butter (pitiful-hearted Titan!) that melted at the sweet tale of
115 the sun's? If thou didst, then behold that compound.
116 FALSTAFF You rogue, here's lime in this sack too! There is nothing but roguery to be found in villainous man. Yet a coward is worse than a cup of sack with lime in it – a villainous coward! Go thy ways, old Jack, die when
120 thou wilt; if manhood, good manhood, be not forgot
121 upon the face of the earth, then am I a shotten herring.

96 *parcel* details 98 *me* (redundant: ethical dative) 102 *drench* dose of medicine; *says he* (i.e. to a servant) 105 *brawn* fat pig 106 *Rivo* (perhaps) bottoms up 108 *of* on 110 *sew netherstocks* a menial occupation 112 *virtue* valor 113 *Titan* the sun 115 *compound* (sweating) lump of butter 116 *lime* added surreptitiously to wine to make it sparkle 120 *manhood* valor 121 *shotten herring* a herring that has deposited its roe

There lives not three good men unhanged in England;
and one of them is fat, and grows old. God help the
while! A bad world, I say. I would I were a weaver; I *124*
could sing psalms or anything. A plague of all cowards, I *125*
say still!

PRINCE How now, woolsack? What mutter you?

FALSTAFF A king's son! If I do not beat thee out of thy
kingdom with a dagger of lath and drive all thy subjects
afore thee like a flock of wild geese, I'll never wear hair
on my face more. You Prince of Wales?

PRINCE Why, you whoreson round man, what's the
matter?

FALSTAFF Are not you a coward? Answer me to that –
and Poins there?

POINS Zounds, ye fat paunch, an ye call me coward, by
the Lord, I'll stab thee.

FALSTAFF I call thee coward? I'll see thee damned ere I
call thee coward, but I would give a thousand pound I
could run as fast as thou canst. You are straight enough
in the shoulders; you care not who sees your back. Call *140*
you that backing of your friends? A plague upon such
backing! Give me them that will face me. Give me a
cup of sack. I am a rogue if I drunk to-day.

PRINCE O villain! thy lips are scarce wiped since thou
drunk'st last.

FALSTAFF All is one for that. *(He drinketh.)* A plague of *146*
all cowards, still say I.

PRINCE What's the matter?

FALSTAFF What's the matter? There be four of us here
have ta'en a thousand pound this day morning.

PRINCE Where is it, Jack? where is it?

FALSTAFF Where is it? Taken from us it is. A hundred
upon poor four of us!

PRINCE What, a hundred, man?

---

124 *while* present time 125 *sing psalms* a habit for which the weavers were
notorious 146 *All...that* it makes no difference

155 FALSTAFF I am a rogue if I were not at half-sword with a
dozen of them two hours together. I have scaped by
miracle. I am eight times thrust through the doublet,
four through the hose; my buckler cut through and
159 through; my sword hacked like a handsaw – ecce sig-
160 num! I never dealt better since I was a man. All would
not do. A plague of all cowards! Let them speak. If they
speak more or less than truth, they are villains and the
sons of darkness.

PRINCE Speak, sirs. How was it?

GADSHILL We four set upon some dozen –

FALSTAFF Sixteen at least, my lord.

GADSHILL And bound them.

PETO No, no, they were not bound.

FALSTAFF You rogue, they were bound, every man of
them, or I am a Jew else – an Ebrew Jew.

GADSHILL As we were sharing, some six or seven fresh
men set upon us –

FALSTAFF And unbound the rest, and then come in the
173 other.

PRINCE What, fought you with them all?

FALSTAFF All? I know not what you call all, but if I
fought not with fifty of them, I am a bunch of radish! If
177 there were not two or three and fifty upon poor old
Jack, then am I no two-legged creature.

PRINCE Pray God you have not murd'red some of
them.

180 FALSTAFF Nay, that's past praying for. I have peppered
181 two of them. Two I am sure I have paid, two rogues in
buckram suits. I tell thee what, Hal – if I tell thee a lie,
spit in my face, call me horse. Thou knowest my old
184 ward. Here I lay, and thus I bore my point. Four

---

155 *at half-sword* at close quarters   159 *ecce signum* look at the evidence
160 *dealt* dealt blows   173 *other* others   177 *three and fifty* the number of
Spanish ships engaged by Sir Richard Grenville in the *Revenge* (1591)   180
peppered made it hot for   181 *paid* i.e. killed   184 *ward* defensive stance;
lay stood

rogues in buckram let drive at me.

PRINCE What, four? Thou saidst but two even now.

FALSTAFF Four, Hal. I told thee four.

POINS Ay, ay, he said four.

FALSTAFF These four came all afront and mainly thrust 189
at me. I made me no more ado but took all their seven 190
points in my target, thus.   191

PRINCE Seven? Why, there were but four even now.

FALSTAFF In buckram?

POINS Ay, four, in buckram suits.

FALSTAFF Seven, by these hilts, or I am a villain else.   195

PRINCE [aside to Poins] Prithee let him alone. We shall
have more anon.

FALSTAFF Dost thou hear me, Hal?

PRINCE Ay, and mark thee too, Jack.

FALSTAFF Do so, for it is worth the list'ning to. These
nine in buckram that I told thee of –

PRINCE So, two more already.

FALSTAFF Their points being broken –   203

POINS Down fell their hose.

FALSTAFF Began to give me ground; but I followed me
close, came in, foot and hand, and with a thought seven 206
of the eleven I paid.

PRINCE O monstrous! Eleven buckram men grown out of 208
two!

FALSTAFF But, as the devil would have it, three mis-
begotten knaves in Kendal green came at my back and
let drive at me; for it was so dark, Hal, that thou couldst
not see thy hand.

PRINCE These lies are like their father that begets them –
gross as a mountain, open, palpable. Why, thou clay-
brained guts, thou knotty-pated fool, thou whoreson 216

---

189 *afront* abreast; *mainly* violently   190 *me* (ethical dative)   191 *target*
shield   195 *villain* no gentleman   203 *points* (1) sword-points, (2) laces
which hold up the clothes   206 *came in* advanced; *with a thought* as quick
as thought   208 *monstrous* astounding   216 *knotty-pated* thick-headed

217 obscene greasy tallow-catch –

FALSTAFF What, art thou mad? art thou mad? Is not the truth the truth?

PRINCE Why, how couldst thou know these men in Kendal green when it was so dark thou couldst not see thy hand? Come, tell us your reason. What sayest thou to this?

POINS Come, your reason, Jack, your reason.

FALSTAFF What, upon compulsion? Zounds, an I were
225 at the strappado or all the racks in the world, I would not tell you on compulsion. Give you a reason on compul-
227 sion? If reasons were as plentiful as blackberries, I would give no man a reason upon compulsion, I.

229 PRINCE I'll be no longer guilty of this sin; this sanguine coward, this bed-presser, this horseback-breaker, this huge hill of flesh –

FALSTAFF 'Sblood, you starveling, you eel-skin, you
233 dried neat's-tongue, you bull's pizzle, you stockfish – O for breath to utter what is like thee! – you tailor's yard,
235 you sheath, you bowcase, you vile standing tuck!

236 PRINCE Well, breathe awhile, and then to it again; and when thou hast tired thyself in base comparisons, hear me speak but this.

POINS Mark, Jack.

PRINCE We two saw you four set on four, and bound them and were masters of their wealth. Mark now how a plain tale shall put you down. Then did we two set on
243 you four and, with a word, outfaced you from your prize, and have it; yea, and can show it you here in the house. And, Falstaff, you carried your guts away as nimbly, with as quick dexterity, and roared for mercy, and still run and roared, as ever I heard bullcalf. What a slave art thou to hack thy sword as thou hast done, and

217 *tallow-catch* tub or lump of tallow   225 *strappado* kind of torture   227 *reasons* (pronounced like 'raisins')   229 *sanguine* daring   233 *stockfish* dried cod   235 *standing tuck* unpliant rapier   236 *breathe* catch your breath; *to it* go to it   243 *with a word* in short; *outfaced* frightened away

then say it was in fight! What trick, what device, what
starting hole canst thou now find out to hide thee from 250
this open and apparent shame?

POINS Come, let's hear, Jack. What trick hast thou now?

FALSTAFF By the Lord, I knew ye as well as he that made
ye. Why, hear you, my masters. Was it for me to kill the
heir apparent? Should I turn upon the true prince?
Why, thou knowest I am as valiant as Hercules, but
beware instinct. The lion will not touch the true prince. 257
Instinct is a great matter. I was now a coward on instinct.
I shall think the better of myself, and thee, during my
life – I for a valiant lion, and thou for a true prince. But,
by the Lord, lads, I am glad you have the money. Hostess, clap to the doors. Watch to-night, pray to-morrow. 262
Gallants, lads, boys, hearts of gold, all the titles of good
fellowship come to you! What, shall we be merry? Shall
we have a play extempore?

PRINCE Content – and the argument shall be thy running 266
away.

FALSTAFF Ah, no more of that, Hal, an thou lovest me!
      Enter Hostess.

HOSTESS O Jesu, my lord the Prince!

PRINCE How now, my lady the hostess? What say'st
thou to me?

HOSTESS Marry, my lord, there is a noble man of the
court at door would speak with you. He says he comes
from your father.

PRINCE Give him as much as will make him a royal man, 275
and send him back again to my mother.

FALSTAFF What manner of man is he?

HOSTESS An old man.

FALSTAFF What doth gravity out of his bed at midnight?
Shall I give him his answer?

---

250 *starting hole* subterfuge, (literally) refuge for hunted animals   **257**
beware take heed of   **262** *Watch . . . to-morrow* cf. 'Watch and pray, that ye
enter not into temptation' (Matthew xxvi, 41)   **266** *argument* subject   **275**
a royal man i.e. worth 10 shillings (3s. 4d. more than a noble)

PRINCE Prithee do, Jack.

FALSTAFF Faith, and I'll send him packing.   *Exit*.

283 **PRINCE** Now, sirs. By'r Lady, you fought fair; so did you, Peto; so did you, Bardolph. You are lions too, you ran away upon instinct, you will not touch the true prince; no – fie!

BARDOLPH Faith, I ran when I saw others run.

PRINCE Tell me now in earnest, how came Falstaff's sword so hacked?

PETO Why, he hacked it with his dagger, and said he
291 would swear truth out of England but he would make you believe it was done in fight, and persuaded us to do the like.

BARDOLPH Yea, and to tickle our noses with speargrass to make them bleed, and then to beslubber our garments
295 with it and swear it was the blood of true men. I did that I did not this seven year before – I blushed to hear his monstrous devices.

PRINCE O villain! thou stolest a cup of sack eighteen years
299 ago and wert taken with the manner, and ever since thou
300 hast blushed extempore. Thou hadst fire and sword on thy side, and yet thou ran'st away. What instinct hadst thou for it?

303 **BARDOLPH** My lord, do you see these meteors? Do you behold these exhalations?

PRINCE I do.

BARDOLPH What think you they portend?

307 **PRINCE** Hot livers and cold purses.

308 **BARDOLPH** Choler, my lord, if rightly taken.

309 **PRINCE** No, if rightly taken, halter.

                 Enter Falstaff.

---

283 *fair* well   291 *but he would* if he did not   295 *true* law-abiding; *that what*   299 *taken . . . manner* caught with the goods   300 *fire* i.e. a red nose and cheeks   303 *meteors* i.e. the red blotches on his face   307 *Hot livers* the effect of drinking   308 *Choler* a choleric (aggressive) disposition; *rightly taken* rightly understood   309 *rightly taken* well captured; *halter* i.e. collar

Here comes lean Jack; here comes bare-bone. How now,
my sweet creature of bombast? How long is't ago, Jack, 311
since thou sawest thine own knee?

FALSTAFF My own knee? When I was about thy years,
Hal, I was not an eagle's talent in the waist; I could have 314
crept into any alderman's thumb-ring. A plague of
sighing and grief! It blows a man up like a bladder. 316
There's villainous news abroad. Here was Sir John
Bracy from your father. You must to the court in the
morning. That same mad fellow of the north, Percy, and
he of Wales that gave Amamon the bastinado, and 320
made Lucifer cuckold, and swore the devil his true 321
liegeman upon the cross of a Welsh hook – what a
plague call you him?

POINS Owen Glendower.

FALSTAFF Owen, Owen – the same; and his son-in-law
Mortimer, and old Northumberland, and that sprightly
Scot of Scots, Douglas, that runs a-horseback up a hill
perpendicular –

PRINCE He that rides at high speed and with his pistol
kills a sparrow flying.

FALSTAFF You have hit it.

PRINCE So did he never the sparrow.

FALSTAFF Well, that rascal hath good metal in him; he 332
will not run. 333

PRINCE Why, what a rascal art thou then, to praise him
so for running!

FALSTAFF A-horseback, ye cuckoo! but afoot he will not
budge a foot.

PRINCE Yes, Jack, upon instinct.

FALSTAFF I grant ye, upon instinct. Well, he is there too,
and one Mordake, and a thousand bluecaps more. 340
Worcester is stol'n away to-night; thy father's beard is

---

311 *bombast* cotton padding   314 *talent* talon   316 *blows . . . up* (actually it
was supposed to make him waste away)   320 *Amamon* a devil; *bastinado*
beating on the soles of the feet   321 *made . . . cuckold* i.e. gave him his horns
332 *metal* material   333 *run* (1) run away, (2) melt   340 *bluecaps* Scots

turned white with the news; you may buy land now as cheap as stinking mack'rel.

PRINCE Why then, it is like, if there come a hot June, and this civil buffeting hold, we shall buy maidenheads as they buy hobnails, by the hundreds.

FALSTAFF By the mass, lad, thou sayest true; it is like we shall have good trading that way. But tell me, Hal, art not thou horrible afeard? Thou being heir apparent,
351 could the world pick thee out three such enemies again as that fiend Douglas, that spirit Percy, and that devil Glendower? Art thou not horribly afraid? Doth not thy
353 blood thrill at it?

PRINCE Not a whit, i' faith. I lack some of thy instinct.

FALSTAFF Well, thou wilt be horribly chid to-morrow when thou comest to thy father. If thou love me, practise an answer.

PRINCE Do thou stand for my father and examine me upon the particulars of my life.

360 FALSTAFF Shall I? Content. This chair shall be my state, this dagger my sceptre, and this cushion my crown.

362 PRINCE Thy state is taken for a joined-stool, thy golden sceptre for a leaden dagger, and thy precious rich crown for a pitiful bald crown.

FALSTAFF Well, an the fire of grace be not quite out of thee, now shalt thou be moved. Give me a cup of sack to make my eyes look red, that it may be thought I have wept; for I must speak in passion, and I will do it in
369 King Cambyses' vein.

370 PRINCE Well, here is my leg.

FALSTAFF And here is my speech. Stand aside, nobility.

HOSTESS O Jesu, this is excellent sport, i' faith!

FALSTAFF
Weep not, sweet queen, for trickling tears are vain.

374 HOSTESS O, the Father, how he holds his countenance!

351 *spirit* evil spirit   353 *thrill* run cold   360 *state* chair of state   362 *taken for* understood to be   369 *King Cambyses' vein* that of an early ranting tragedy   370 *leg* bow   374 *holds his countenance* keeps a straight face

FALSTAFF
   For God's sake, lords, convey my tristful queen!   375
   For tears do stop the floodgates of her eyes.

HOSTESS O Jesu, he doth it as like one of these harlotry 377
   players as ever I see!

FALSTAFF Peace, good pintpot. Peace, good tickle-
   brain. – Harry, I do not only marvel where thou spend-
   est thy time, but also how thou art accompanied. For
   though the camomile, the more it is trodden on, the
   faster it grows, yet youth, the more it is wasted, the
   sooner it wears. That thou art my son I have partly thy
   mother's word, partly my own opinion, but chiefly a
   villainous trick of thine eye and a foolish hanging of thy 386
   nether lip that doth warrant me. If then thou be son to 387
   me, here lies the point: why, being son to me, art thou
   so pointed at? Shall the blessed sun of heaven prove a
   micher and eat blackberries? A question not to be 390
   asked. Shall the son of England prove a thief and take
   purses? A question to be asked. There is a thing, Harry,
   which thou hast often heard of, and it is known to many
   in our land by the name of pitch. This pitch, as ancient 394
   writers do report, doth defile; so doth the company thou
   keepest. For, Harry, now I do not speak to thee in
   drink, but in tears; not in pleasure, but in passion; not
   in words only, but in woes also: and yet there is a virtuous man whom I have often noted in thy company, but
   I know not his name.

PRINCE What manner of man, an it like your majesty?

FALSTAFF A goodly portly man, i' faith, and a corpulent; 401
   of a cheerful look, a pleasing eye, and a most noble
   carriage; and, as I think, his age some fifty, or, by'r
   Lady, inclining to threescore; and now I remember me,
   his name is Falstaff. If that man should be lewdly given, 405

---

375 *convey* escort hence; *tristful* sorrowful   377 *harlotry* scurvy   386 *trick*
peculiarity   387 *warrant* assure   390 *micher* truant   394–95 *ancient
writers* i.e. Ecclesiasticus xiii, 1   401 *goodly* handsome; *portly* dignified
405 *lewdly* wickedly

he deceiveth me; for, Harry, I see virtue in his looks. If
407 then the tree may be known by the fruit, as the fruit by
408 the tree, then, peremptorily I speak it, there is virtue in
that Falstaff. Him keep with, the rest banish. And tell
410 me now, thou naughty varlet, tell me where hast thou
been this month?

PRINCE Dost thou speak like a king? Do thou stand for
me, and I'll play my father.

FALSTAFF Depose me? If thou dost it half so gravely, so
majestically, both in word and matter, hang me up by
415 the heels for a rabbit-sucker or a poulter's hare.

PRINCE Well, here I am set.

FALSTAFF And here I stand. Judge, my masters.

PRINCE Now, Harry, whence come you?

FALSTAFF My noble lord, from Eastcheap.

PRINCE The complaints I hear of thee are grievous.

FALSTAFF 'Sblood, my lord, they are false! Nay, I'll
422 tickle ye for a young prince, i' faith.

423 PRINCE Swearest thou, ungracious boy? Henceforth
ne'er look on me. Thou art violently carried away from
grace. There is a devil haunts thee in the likeness of an
old fat man; a tun of man is thy companion. Why dost
427 thou converse with that trunk of humors, that bolting
hutch of beastliness, that swoll'n parcel of dropsies, that
429 huge bombard of sack, that stuffed cloakbag of guts,
430 that roasted Manningtree ox with the pudding in his
431 belly, that reverend vice, that grey iniquity, that father
432 ruffian, that vanity in years? Wherein is he good, but to
433 taste sack and drink it? wherein neat and cleanly, but to
434 carve a capon and eat it? wherein cunning, but in craft?

---

407 *tree . . . by the fruit* cf. Matthew xii, 33   **408** *peremptorily* positively   **410**
varlet rascal   **415** *rabbit-sucker* very young rabbit   **422** *tickle . . . prince*
divert you in the role of a young prince   **423** *ungracious* graceless   **427**
converse associate; *humors* fluids of the body   **427–28** *bolting hutch* large
flour bin   **429** *bombard* leather vessel   **430** *Manningtree ox* famous for size;
pudding stuffing   **431** *vice* chief comic character and mischief-maker of the
moral plays   **432** *vanity* (incarnation of) worldliness   **433** *cleanly* deft
434 *cunning* skillful

wherein crafty, but in villainy? wherein villainous, but in all things? wherein worthy, but in nothing?

FALSTAFF I would your grace would take me with you. 437
Whom means your grace?

PRINCE That villainous abominable misleader of youth, Falstaff, that old white-bearded Satan.

FALSTAFF My lord, the man I know.

PRINCE I know thou dost.

FALSTAFF But to say I know more harm in him than in myself were to say more than I know. That he is old (the more the pity), his white hairs do witness it; but that he is (saving your reverence) a whoremaster, that I utterly 446
deny. If sack and sugar be a fault, God help the wicked! If to be old and merry be a sin, then many an old host that I know is damned. If to be fat be to be hated, then Pharaoh's lean kine are to be loved. No, my good lord: 450
banish Peto, banish Bardolph, banish Poins; but for sweet Jack Falstaff, kind Jack Falstaff, true Jack Falstaff, valiant Jack Falstaff, and therefore more valiant being, as he is, old Jack Falstaff, banish not him thy Harry's company, banish not him thy Harry's company. Banish plump Jack, and banish all the world!

PRINCE I do, I will.
    [A knocking heard.]
            [Exeunt Hostess, Francis, and Bardolph.]
    Enter Bardolph, running.

BARDOLPH O, my lord, my lord! the sheriff with a most monstrous watch is at the door. 459

FALSTAFF Out, ye rogue! Play out the play. I have much to say in the behalf of that Falstaff.
    Enter the Hostess.

HOSTESS O Jesu, my lord, my lord!

PRINCE Heigh, heigh, the devil rides upon a fiddlestick! 463
What's the matter?

---

437 *take . . . you* make yourself clear   446 *saving your reverence* excuse my speaking plainly   450 *kine* cf. Genesis xli, 18–21   459 *watch* posse of watchmen (constables)   463 *the devil . . . fiddlestick* much ado about nothing

HOSTESS The sheriff and all the watch are at the door.
They are come to search the house. Shall I let them in?

467 FALSTAFF Dost thou hear, Hal? Never call a true piece of
gold a counterfeit. Thou art essentially mad without
seeming so.

PRINCE And thou a natural coward without instinct.

471 FALSTAFF I deny your major. If you will deny the sheriff,
472 so; if not, let him enter. If I become not a cart as well as
another man, a plague on my bringing up! I hope I shall
474 as soon be strangled with a halter as another.

475 PRINCE Go hide thee behind the arras. The rest walk up
476 above. Now, my masters, for a true face and good conscience.

478 FALSTAFF Both which I have had; but their date is out,
and therefore I'll hide me.   _Exit._

PRINCE Call in the sheriff.
                                   [Exeunt. Manent the Prince and Peto.]
                                   Enter Sheriff and the Carrier.

Now, master sheriff, what is your will with me?

SHERIFF
First, pardon me, my lord. A hue and cry
Hath followed certain men unto this house.

PRINCE
What men?

SHERIFF
One of them is well known, my gracious lord –
A gross fat man.

CARRIER   As fat as butter.

PRINCE
The man, I do assure you, is not here,
For I myself at this time have employed him.
489 And, sheriff, I will engage my word to thee

467–69 _Never . . . so_ (perhaps) you are crazy to banish such a sterling
fellow as plump Jack   471 _major_ (1) major premise, (2) mayor   472 _cart_
(in which criminals were carried to execution)   474 _soon_ quickly   475 _arras_
tapestry which screened the walls   476 _true_ honest   478 _date is out_ term
has expired   489 _engage_ pledge

That I will by to-morrow dinner time
Send him to answer thee, or any man,
For anything he shall be charged withal;
And so let me entreat you leave the house.

SHERIFF
I will, my lord. There are two gentlemen
Have in this robbery lost three hundred marks.

PRINCE
It may be so. If he have robbed these men,
He shall be answerable; and so farewell.

SHERIFF
Good night, my noble lord.

PRINCE
I think it is good morrow, is it not?   499

SHERIFF
Indeed, my lord, I think it be two o'clock.
                                    Exit [with Carrier].

PRINCE This oily rascal is known as well as Paul's. Go 501
call him forth.

PETO Falstaff! Fast asleep behind the arras, and snorting
like a horse.

PRINCE Hark how hard he fetches breath. Search his
pockets.
    He searcheth his pockets and findeth certain papers.
What hast thou found?

PETO Nothing but papers, my lord.

PRINCE Let's see what they be. Read them.

PETO *[reads]* 'Item, A capon   .   .   .   ii s. ii d.
            Item, Sauce .   .   .   .   iiii d.
            Item, Sack two gallons   .   v s. viii d.
            Item, Anchovies and sack after
                supper   .   .   .   ii s. vi d.
            Item, Bread   .   .   .   ob.' 513

PRINCE O monstrous! but one halfpennyworth of bread 514

---

499 *morrow* morning   501 *Paul's* St Paul's Cathedral, the center of London
life   513 *ob.* obolus, halfpenny   514 *monstrous* astounding

to this intolerable deal of sack! What there is else, keep
516 close; we'll read it at more advantage. There let him
sleep till day. I'll to the court in the morning. We must
all to the wars, and thy place shall be honorable. I'll
519 procure this fat rogue a charge of foot, and I know his
520 death will be a march of twelve score. The money shall be
521 paid back again with advantage. Be with me betimes in
the morning, and so good morrow, Peto.

PETO Good morrow, good my lord.   *Exeunt.*

*

III, i   *Enter Hotspur, Worcester, Lord Mortimer, Owen
Glendower.*

MORTIMER
These promises are fair, the parties sure,
2   And our induction full of prosperous hope.

HOTSPUR Lord Mortimer, and cousin Glendower, will
you sit down? And uncle Worcester. A plague upon it! I
have forgot the map.

GLENDOWER
No, here it is. Sit, cousin Percy;
Sit, good cousin Hotspur, for by that name
8   As oft as Lancaster doth speak of you,
His cheek looks pale, and with a rising sigh
He wisheth you in heaven.

HOTSPUR And you in hell, as oft as he hears Owen
Glendower spoke of.

GLENDOWER
I cannot blame him. At my nativity

---

516 *close* to yourself; *advantage* favorable opportunity   519 *a charge of foot*
command of a company of infantry   520 *twelve score* i.e. yards   521
advantage interest
III, i Within Glendower's castle in Wales (Holinshed names as the meeting-
place the Archdeacon's house at Bangor, but in the play Glendower is
acting as host)   2 *induction* first step; *prosperous hope* hope of prospering
8 *Lancaster* i.e. the king

The front of heaven was full of fiery shapes   14
Of burning cressets, and at my birth   15
The frame and huge foundation of the earth
Shaked like a coward.

HOTSPUR Why, so it would have done at the same season
    if your mother's cat had but kittened, though yourself
    had never been born.

GLENDOWER
    I say the earth did shake when I was born.

HOTSPUR
    And I say the earth was not of my mind,
    If you suppose as fearing you it shook.

GLENDOWER
    The heavens were all on fire, the earth did tremble.

HOTSPUR
    O, then the earth shook to see the heavens on fire,
    And not in fear of your nativity.
    Diseasèd nature oftentimes breaks forth
    In strange eruptions; oft the teeming earth
    Is with a kind of colic pinched and vexed
    By the imprisoning of unruly wind
    Within her womb, which, for enlargement striving,   31
    Shakes the old beldame earth and topples down   32
    Steeples and mossgrown towers. At your birth
    Our grandam earth, having this distemp'rature,   34
    In passion shook.   35

GLENDOWER   Cousin, of many men
    I do not bear these crossings. Give me leave   36
    To tell you once again that at my birth
    The front of heaven was full of fiery shapes,
    The goats ran from the mountains, and the herds
    Were strangely clamorous to the frighted fields.
    These signs have marked me extraordinary,
    And all the courses of my life do show

14 *front* forehead   15 *cressets* lights burning in baskets mounted on poles
31 *enlargement* release   32 *beldame* grandmother   34 *distemp'rature* ailment
35 *passion* pain   36 *crossings* contradictions

I am not in the roll of common men.

44 Where is he living, clipped in with the sea

45 That chides the banks of England, Scotland, Wales,

46 Which calls me pupil or hath read to me?

And bring him out that is but woman's son

48 Can trace me in the tedious ways of art

49 And hold me pace in deep experiments.

50 HOTSPUR I think there's no man speaks better Welsh.
I'll to dinner.

MORTIMER
Peace, cousin Percy; you will make him mad.

GLENDOWER

53 I can call spirits from the vasty deep.

HOTSPUR
Why, so can I, or so can any man;
But will they come when you do call for them?

GLENDOWER Why, I can teach you, cousin, to command
the devil.

HOTSPUR
And I can teach thee, coz, to shame the devil –
By telling truth. Tell truth and shame the devil.
If thou have power to raise him, bring him hither,
And I'll be sworn I have power to shame him hence.
O, while you live, tell truth and shame the devil!

MORTIMER
Come, come, no more of this unprofitable chat.

GLENDOWER

64 Three times hath Henry Bolingbroke made head
Against my power; thrice from the banks of Wye
And sandy-bottomed Severn have I sent him

67 Booteless home and weather-beaten back.

HOTSPUR
Home without boots, and in foul weather too?

---

44 *clipped in with* enclosed by   45 *chides* lashes   46 *read to* instructed   48 *trace* follow; *tedious* laborious; *art* i.e. magic   49 *hold me pace* keep pace with me; *deep* occult   50 *Welsh* i.e. bragging   53 *vasty deep* abyss of the lower world   64 *made head* raised troops   67 *Booteless* without advantage

How scapes he agues, in the devil's name? 69

GLENDOWER

Come, here is the map. Shall we divide our right 70
According to our threefold order ta'en? 71

MORTIMER

The archdeacon hath divided it
Into three limits very equally. 73
England, from Trent and Severn hitherto, 74
By south and east is to my part assigned;
All westward, Wales beyond the Severn shore,
And all the fertile land within that bound,
To Owen Glendower; and, dear coz, to you
The remnant northward lying off from Trent. 79
And our indentures tripartite are drawn, 80
Which being sealèd interchangeably
(A business that this night may execute),
To-morrow, cousin Percy, you and I
And my good Lord of Worcester will set forth
To meet your father and the Scottish power,
As is appointed us, at Shrewsbury.
My father Glendower is not ready yet, 87
Nor shall we need his help these fourteen days.
    [To Glendower]
Within that space you may have drawn together 89
Your tenants, friends, and neighboring gentlemen.

GLENDOWER

A shorter time shall send me to you, lords;
And in my conduct shall your ladies come,
From whom you now must steal and take no leave,
For there will be a world of water shed
Upon the parting of your wives and you.

HOTSPUR

Methinks my moiety, north from Burton here, 96

69 *agues* malaria 70 *right* rightful possessions 71 *order* arrangement 73
limits territories 74 *hitherto* to this spot 79 *lying off* starting 80 *tripartite* i.e. in triplicate; *drawn* drawn up 87 *father* i.e. father-in-law 89
may will be able to 96 *moiety* share

81

In quantity equals not one of yours.

98 See how this river comes me cranking in
And cuts me from the best of all my land

100 A huge half-moon, a monstrous cantle out.
I'll have the current in this place dammed up,

102 And here the smug and silver Trent shall run

103 In a new channel fair and evenly.
It shall not wind with such a deep indent

105 To rob me of so rich a bottom here.

GLENDOWER
Not wind? It shall, it must! You see it doth.

MORTIMER
Yea, but
Mark how he bears his course, and runs me up
With like advantage on the other side,

110 Gelding the opposèd continent as much
As on the other side it takes from you.

WORCESTER

112 Yea, but a little charge will trench him here
And on this north side win this cape of land;
And then he runs straight and even.

HOTSPUR
I'll have it so. A little charge will do it.

GLENDOWER
I will not have it alt'red.

HOTSPUR   Will not you?

GLENDOWER
No, nor you shall not.

HOTSPUR   Who shall say me nay?

GLENDOWER
Why, that will I.

HOTSPUR
Let me not understand you then; speak it in Welsh.

98 *cranking* winding   100 *cantle* hunk   102 *smug* smooth   103 *fair* gently
105 *bottom* valley   110 *continent* land which it bounds   112 *charge* expendi-
ture; *trench* dig a new channel

GLENDOWER

I can speak English, lord, as well as you;
For I was trained up in the English court,
Where, being but young, I framèd to the harp
Many an English ditty lovely well,
And gave the tongue a helpful ornament –   124
A virtue that was never seen in you.   125

HOTSPUR

Marry, and I am glad of it with all my heart!
I had rather be a kitten and cry mew
Than one of these same metre ballet-mongers.   128
I had rather hear a brazen canstick turned   129
Or a dry wheel grate on the axletree,
And that would set my teeth nothing on edge,
Nothing so much as mincing poetry.
'Tis like the forced gait of a shuffling nag.   133

GLENDOWER

Come, you shall have Trent turned.

HOTSPUR

I do not care. I'll give thrice so much land
To any well-deserving friend;
But in the way of bargain, mark ye me,
I'll cavil on the ninth part of a hair.
Are the indentures drawn? Shall we be gone?

GLENDOWER

The moon shines fair; you may away by night.
I'll haste the writer, and withal
Break with your wives of your departure hence.   142
I am afraid my daughter will run mad,
So much she doteth on her Mortimer.   *Exit.*

MORTIMER

Fie, cousin Percy! how you cross my father!

HOTSPUR

I cannot choose. Sometimes he angers me

124 *tongue* i.e. words; *ornament* i.e. music   125 *virtue* accomplishment
128 *ballet-mongers* ballad-makers   129 *canstick* candlestick   133 *shuffling*
hobbled   142 *Break with* inform

147 With telling me of the moldwarp and the ant,
   Of the dreamer Merlin and his prophecies,
   And of a dragon and a finless fish,
150 A clip-winged griffin and a moulten raven,
151 A couching lion and a ramping cat,
152 And such a deal of skimble-skamble stuff
153 As puts me from my faith. I tell you what –
   He held me last night at least nine hours
155 In reckoning up the several devils' names
156 That were his lackeys. I cried 'hum,' and 'well, go to!'
   But marked him not a word. O, he is as tedious
   As a tired horse, a railing wife;
   Worse than a smoky house. I had rather live
   With cheese and garlic in a windmill far
161 Than feed on cates and have him talk to me
   In any summer house in Christendom.

MORTIMER
   In faith, he is a worthy gentleman,
164 Exceedingly well read, and profited
165 In strange concealments, valiant as a lion,
   And wondrous affable, and as bountiful
   As mines of India. Shall I tell you, cousin?
   He holds your temper in a high respect
169 And curbs himself even of his natural scope
   When you come 'cross his humor. Faith, he does.
   I warrant you that man is not alive
172 Might so have tempted him as you have done
   Without the taste of danger and reproof.
174 But do not use it oft, let me entreat you.

WORCESTER
175 In faith, my lord, you are too willful-blame,

---

147 *moldwarp* mole 150 *griffin* half lion, half eagle 151 *couching* crouching; *ramping* rearing on hind legs 152 *skimble-skamble* nonsensical 153 *puts* forces 155 *several* different 156 *go to* 'you don't say' 161 *cates* delicacies 164 *profited* proficient 165 *concealments* secrets 169 *scope* freedom of speech 172 *tempted* provoked 174 *use* do 175 *willful-blame* willfully blamable

And since your coming hither have done enough
To put him quite besides his patience.   177
You must needs learn, lord, to amend this fault.
Though sometimes it show greatness, courage, blood –   179
And that's the dearest grace it renders you –   180
Yet oftentimes it doth present harsh rage,   181
Defect of manners, want of government,
Pride, haughtiness, opinion, and disdain;   183
The least of which haunting a nobleman
Loseth men's hearts, and leaves behind a stain
Upon the beauty of all parts besides,   186
Beguiling them of commendation.   187

HOTSPUR
Well, I am schooled. Good manners be your speed!   188
Here come our wives, and let us take our leave.
Enter Glendower with the Ladies.

MORTIMER
This is the deadly spite that angers me –   190
My wife can speak no English, I no Welsh.

GLENDOWER
My daughter weeps; she will not part with you;
She'll be a soldier too, she'll to the wars.

MORTIMER
Good father, tell her that she and my aunt Percy   194
Shall follow in your conduct speedily.
*Glendower speaks to her in Welsh, and she answers
him in the same.*

GLENDOWER
She is desperate here. A peevish self-willed harlotry,   196
One that no persuasion can do good upon.
The Lady speaks in Welsh.

---

177 *besides* out of   **179** *blood* spirit   **180** *dearest grace* best credit   **181** *present* represent   **183** *opinion* arrogance   **186** *parts* abilities   **187** *Beguiling* robbing   **188** *be your speed* give you good fortune   **190** *spite* vexation   **194** *aunt* (to Edmund Mortimer, Earl of March, but sister-in-law to Glendower's son-in-law)   **196** *here* on this point; *peevish* childish; *harlotry* silly wench

MORTIMER

I understand thy looks. That pretty Welsh

199 Which thou pourest down from these swelling heavens

200 I am too perfect in; and, but for shame,

201 In such a parley should I answer thee.
                The Lady again in Welsh.
I understand thy kisses, and thou mine,

203 And that's a feeling disputation.
But I will never be a truant, love,
Till I have learnt thy language; for thy tongue

206 Makes Welsh as sweet as ditties highly penned,
Sung by a fair queen in a summer's bow'r,

208 With ravishing division, to her lute.

GLENDOWER

Nay, if you melt, then will she run mad.
                The Lady speaks again in Welsh.

MORTIMER

O, I am ignorance itself in this!

GLENDOWER

211 She bids you on the wanton rushes lay you down
And rest your gentle head upon her lap,
And she will sing the song that pleaseth you
And on your eyelids crown the god of sleep,

215 Charming your blood with pleasing heaviness,
Making such difference 'twixt wake and sleep
As is the difference betwixt day and night
The hour before the heavenly-harnessed team
Begins his golden progress in the east.

MORTIMER

With all my heart I'll sit and hear her sing.

221 By that time will our book, I think, be drawn.

GLENDOWER

Do so, and those musicians that shall play to you
Hang in the air a thousand leagues from hence,

---

199 *heavens* i.e. eyes   200 *perfect* proficient   201 *such a parley* the same language   203 *disputation* conversation   206 *highly* nobly   208 *division* melody   211 *wanton* luxurious   215 *blood* mood   221 *book* the indenture

And straight they shall be here. Sit, and attend.

HOTSPUR Come, Kate, thou art perfect in lying down. 225
Come, quick, quick, that I may lay my head in thy lap.

LADY PERCY Go, ye giddy goose.

The music plays.

HOTSPUR

Now I perceive the devil understands Welsh.
And 'tis no marvel he is so humorous,   229
By'r Lady, he is a good musician.

LADY PERCY Then should you be nothing but musical,
for you are altogether governed by humors. Lie still, ye 232
thief, and hear the lady sing in Welsh.

HOTSPUR I had rather hear Lady, my brach, howl in 234
Irish.

LADY PERCY Wouldst thou have thy head broken?

HOTSPUR No.

LADY PERCY Then be still.

HOTSPUR Neither! 'Tis a woman's fault.

LADY PERCY Now God help thee!

HOTSPUR To the Welsh lady's bed.

LADY PERCY What's that?

HOTSPUR Peace! she sings.

Here the Lady sings a Welsh song.

Come, Kate, I'll have your song too.

LADY PERCY Not mine, in good sooth.   244

HOTSPUR Not yours, in good sooth? Heart! you swear
like a comfit-maker's wife. 'Not you, in good sooth!' and 246
'as true as I live!' and 'as God shall mend me!' and 'as
sure as day!'
And givest such sarcenet surety for thy oaths   249
As if thou never walk'st further than Finsbury.   250
Swear me, Kate, like a lady as thou art,   251
A good mouth-filling oath, and leave 'in sooth'

---

225 *perfect* well-trained 229 *humorous* emotional 232 *humors* whims
234 *brach* bitch-hound 244 *sooth* truth 246 *comfit-maker's* confectioner's
249 *sarcenet surety* flimsy confirmation 250 *Finsbury* field near London
frequented by citizens on Sundays 251 *me* (ethical dative)

253   And such protest of pepper gingerbread
254   To velvet guards and Sunday citizens.
       Come, sing.
       LADY PERCY I will not sing.
257 HOTSPUR 'Tis the next way to turn tailor or be red-
       breast-teacher. An the indentures be drawn, I'll away
       within these two hours; and so come in when ye will.
                                                    Exit.

       GLENDOWER
       Come, come, Lord Mortimer. You are as slow
       As hot Lord Percy is on fire to go.
       By this our book is drawn; we'll but seal,
       And then to horse immediately.
       MORTIMER   With all my heart.   *Exeunt.*

                              *

III, ii   *Enter the King, Prince of Wales, and others.*
       KING
       Lords, give us leave: the Prince of Wales and I
       Must have some private conference; but be near at
       hand,
       For we shall presently have need of you.   *Exeunt Lords.*
       I know not whether God will have it so
       For some displeasing service I have done,
6   That, in his secret doom, out of my blood
       He'll breed revengement and a scourge for me ;
8   But thou dost in thy passages of life
9   Make me believe that thou art only marked
       For the hot vengeance and the rod of heaven
       To punish my mistreadings. Tell me else,

---

253 *protest . . . gingerbread* mealy-mouthed swearing   **254** *velvet guards*
(middle-class women dressed up in clothes with) velvet trimmings   **257**
next easiest; *tailor* proverbially a singer   **257–58** *be redbreast-teacher* teach
birds to sing
III, ii Within the palace of King Henry IV   **6** *doom* judgment   **8** *thy . . .
life* the actions of your life   **9–10** *marked For* destined to be

Could such inordinate and low desires, 12
Such poor, such bare, such lewd, such mean attempts, 13
Such barren pleasures, rude society,
As thou art matched withal and grafted to,
Accompany the greatness of thy blood
And hold their level with thy princely heart? 17

PRINCE
So please your majesty, I would I could
Quit all offenses with as clear excuse 19
As well as I am doubtless I can purge 20
Myself of many I am charged withal.
Yet such extenuation let me beg 22
As, in reproof of many tales devised, 23
Which oft the ear of greatness needs must hear
By smiling pickthanks and base newsmongers, 25
I may, for some things true wherein my youth
Hath faulty wand'red and irregular,
Find pardon on my true submission. 28

KING
God pardon thee! Yet let me wonder, Harry,
At thy affections, which do hold a wing 30
Quite from the flight of all thy ancestors. 31
Thy place in council thou hast rudely lost, 32
Which by thy younger brother is supplied,
And art almost an alien to the hearts
Of all the court and princes of my blood.
The hope and expectation of thy time 36
Is ruined, and the soul of every man
Prophetically do forethink thy fall.
Had I so lavish of my presence been,

---

12 *inordinate* beneath your position 13 *lewd* low; *attempts* undertakings
17 *hold . . . with* be on equality with 19 *Quit* acquit myself of 20 *am
doubtless* have no doubt; *purge* acquit 22 *extenuation* mitigation 23 *in
reproof* upon disproof 25 *pickthanks* flatterers; *newsmongers* talebearers
28 *submission* admission of fault 30 *affections* inclinations; *hold a wing*
take a course 31 *from* contrary to 32 *rudely* by violence 36 *time* i.e.
youth

40   So common-hackneyed in the eyes of men,
      So stale and cheap to vulgar company,
42   Opinion, that did help me to the crown,
43   Had still kept loyal to possession
      And left me in reputeless banishment,
      A fellow of no mark nor likelihood.
      By being seldom seen, I could not stir
      But, like a comet, I was wond'red at;
      That men would tell their children, 'This is he!'
      Others would say, 'Where? Which is Bolingbroke?'
50   And then I stole all courtesy from heaven,
      And dressed myself in such humility
      That I did pluck allegiance from men's hearts,
      Loud shouts and salutations from their mouths
      Even in the presence of the crownèd king.
      Thus did I keep my person fresh and new,
      My presence, like a robe pontifical,
57   Ne'er seen but wond'red at; and so my state,
      Seldom but sumptuous, showed like a feast
59   And wan by rareness such solemnity.
60   The skipping king, he ambled up and down
61   With shallow jesters and rash bavin wits,
62   Soon kindled and soon burnt; carded his state;
      Mingled his royalty with cap'ring fools;
64   Had his great name profanèd with their scorns
65   And gave his countenance, against his name,
66   To laugh at gibing boys and stand the push
67   Of every beardless vain comparative;
      Grew a companion to the common streets,
69   Enfeoffed himself to popularity;

---

40 *common-hackneyed* vulgarized   42 *Opinion* i.e. public opinion   43 *Had*
would have; *possession* i.e. the possessor   50 *courtesy* humility   57 *state* i.e.
appearances in state   59 *wan* won; *such solemnity* i.e. that of a festival   60
skipping flighty   61 *rash* quick to burn; *bavin* (literally) brushwood   62
carded mixed with baseness   64 *their scorns* the scorn felt for them   65
name reputation   66 *stand the push* serve as the butt   67 *comparative* wise-
cracker   69 *Enfeoffed* surrendered; *popularity* the populace

That, being daily swallowed by men's eyes,
They surfeited with honey and began
To loathe the taste of sweetness, whereof a little
More than a little is by much too much.
So, when he had occasion to be seen,
He was but as the cuckoo is in June,
Heard, not regarded – seen, but with such eyes
As, sick and blunted with community,   77
Afford no extraordinary gaze,
Such as is bent on sunlike majesty
When it shines seldom in admiring eyes;
But rather drowsed and hung their eyelids down,
Slept in his face, and rend'red such aspect   82
As cloudy men use to their adversaries,   83
Being with his presence glutted, gorged, and full.
And in that very line, Harry, standest thou;   85
For thou hast lost thy princely privilege
With vile participation. Not an eye   87
But is aweary of thy common sight,
Save mine, which hath desired to see thee more;
Which now doth that I would not have it do –
Make blind itself with foolish tenderness.

PRINCE
I shall hereafter, my thrice-gracious lord,
Be more myself.

KING   For all the world,
As thou art to this hour was Richard then
When I from France set foot at Ravenspurgh;
And even as I was then is Percy now.
Now, by my sceptre, and my soul to boot,
He hath more worthy interest to the state   98
Than thou, the shadow of succession;   99
For of no right, nor color like to right,   100

---

77 *community* commonness 82 *Slept in* disregarded; *aspect* look 83
cloudy sullen 85 *line* station 87 *vile participation* association with the
mean 98 *interest* title 99 *the shadow of succession* a successor with a poor
claim 100 *color* pretext

101   He doth fill fields with harness in the realm,
102   Turns head against the lion's armèd jaws,
    And, being no more in debt to years than thou,
    Leads ancient lords and reverend bishops on
    To bloody battles and to bruising arms.
    What never-dying honor hath he got
    Against renownèd Douglas! whose high deeds,
    Whose hot incursions and great name in arms
109   Holds from all soldiers chief majority
110   And military title capital
    Through all the kingdoms that acknowledge Christ.
    Thrice hath this Hotspur, Mars in swathling clothes,
    This infant warrior, in his enterprises
    Discomfited great Douglas; ta'en him once,
115   Enlargèd him, and made a friend of him,
116   To fill the mouth of deep defiance up
    And shake the peace and safety of our throne.
    And what say you to this? Percy, Northumberland,
    The Archbishop's grace of York, Douglas, Mortimer
120   Capitulate against us and are up.
    But wherefore do I tell these news to thee?
    Why, Harry, do I tell thee of my foes,
    Which art my nearest and dearest enemy?
124   Thou that art like enough, through vassal fear,
125   Base inclination, and the start of spleen,
    To fight against me under Percy's pay,
    To dog his heels and curtsy at his frowns,
    To show how much thou art degenerate.

PRINCE
    Do not think so. You shall not find it so.
    And God forgive them that so much have swayed
    Your majesty's good thoughts away from me.

---

101 *harness* (men in) armor   102 *Turns head* marches with an army; *lion's* i.e. king's   109 *majority* pre-eminence   110 *capital* principal   115 *Enlargèd* set free   116 *fill . . . up* make defiance roar all the more loudly   120 *Capitulate* draw up articles of agreement; *up* in arms   124 *vassal* slavish   125 *Base inclination* inclination towards baseness; *start of spleen* perversity

I will redeem all this on Percy's head 132
And, in the closing of some glorious day,
Be bold to tell you that I am your son,
When I will wear a garment all of blood,
And stain my favors in a bloody mask, 136
Which, washed away, shall scour my shame with it. 137
And that shall be the day, whene'er it lights, 138
That this same child of honor and renown,
This gallant Hotspur, this all-praisèd knight,
And your unthought-of Harry chance to meet.
For every honor sitting on his helm,
Would they were multitudes, and on my head
My shames redoubled! For the time will come
That I shall make this northern youth exchange
His glorious deeds for my indignities. 146
Percy is but my factor, good my lord, 147
To engross up glorious deeds on my behalf; 148
And I will call him to so strict account
That he shall render every glory up,
Yea, even the slightest worship of his time, 151
Or I will tear the reckoning from his heart.
This in the name of God I promise here;
The which if he be pleased I shall perform,
I do beseech your majesty may salve
The long-grown wounds of my intemperance. 156
If not, the end of life cancels all bands, 157
And I will die a hundred thousand deaths
Ere break the smallest parcel of this vow.

KING

A hundred thousand rebels die in this!
Thou shalt have charge and sovereign trust herein. 161
  Enter Blunt.
How now, good Blunt? Thy looks are full of speed.

---

132 *redeem* make up for 136 *favors* features 137 *shame* disgrace 138
lights dawns 146 *indignities* unworthy traits 147 *factor* agent 148
engross up buy up 151 *worship* honor; *time* lifetime 156 *intemperance*
dissolute behavior 157 *bands* bonds 161 *charge* command

BLUNT

163   So hath the business that I come to speak of.
164   Lord Mortimer of Scotland hath sent word
        That Douglas and the English rebels met
        The eleventh of this month at Shrewsbury.
167   A mighty and a fearful head they are,
        If promises be kept on every hand,
        As ever off'red foul play in a state.

KING

        The Earl of Westmoreland set forth to-day;
        With him my son, Lord John of Lancaster;
172   For this advertisement is five days old.
        On Wednesday next, Harry, you shall set forward;
174   On Thursday we ourselves will march. Our meeting
        Is Bridgenorth; and, Harry, you shall march
        Through Gloucestershire; by which account,
177   Our business valuèd, some twelve days hence
        Our general forces at Bridgenorth shall meet.
        Our hands are full of business. Let's away:
180   Advantage feeds him fat while men delay.   *Exeunt.*

*

III, iii   *Enter Falstaff and Bardolph.*

   FALSTAFF Bardolph, am I not fall'n away vilely since
2   this last action? Do I not bate? Do I not dwindle? Why,
        my skin hangs about me like an old lady's loose gown! I
4   am withered like an old apple-john. Well, I'll repent,
5   and that suddenly, while I am in some liking. I shall be

---

163 *hath* i.e. hath speed, is urgent 164 *Lord Mortimer of Scotland* a
Scottish nobleman, no relative of Edmund Mortimer 167 *head* force
172 *advertisement* information 174 *meeting* meeting-place 177 *Our business valuèd* considering how long our business will take 180 *Advantage*
opportunity; *fat* i.e. lazy
III, iii Within an Eastcheap tavern 2 *action* battle, i.e. the robbery; *bate*
grow thin 4 *apple-john* an apple eaten when the skin has shrivelled 5
suddenly immediately; *liking* (1) inclination, (2) good fettle

out of heart shortly, and then I shall have no strength to 6
repent. An I have not forgotten what the inside of a
church is made of, I am a peppercorn, a brewer's horse. 8
The inside of a church! Company, villainous company,
hath been the spoil of me.

BARDOLPH Sir John, you are so fretful you cannot live
long.

FALSTAFF Why, there is it! Come, sing me a bawdy song;
make me merry. I was as virtuously given as a gentleman need to be, virtuous enough: swore little, diced not
above seven times a week, went to a bawdy house not
above once in a quarter of an hour, paid money that I
borrowed three or four times, lived well, and in good
compass; and now I live out of all order, out of all 17
compass.

BARDOLPH Why, you are so fat, Sir John, that you must
needs be out of all compass – out of all reasonable compass, Sir John.

FALSTAFF Do thou amend thy face, and I'll amend my 22
life. Thou art our admiral, thou bearest the lantern in 23
the poop – but 'tis in the nose of thee. Thou art the
Knight of the Burning Lamp.   25

BARDOLPH Why, Sir John, my face does you no harm.

FALSTAFF No, I'll be sworn. I make as good use of it as
many a man doth of a death's-head or a memento mori. 28
I never see thy face but I think upon hellfire and Dives 29
that lived in purple; for there he is in his robes, burning,
burning. If thou wert any way given to virtue, I would
swear by thy face; my oath should be 'By this fire, that's 32

---

6 *out of heart* depressed   8 *peppercorn* berry of pepper; *brewer's horse* i.e.
lean and worn out   17 *compass* (1) limit, (2) girth   22 *face* (which is violently inflamed and pimpled)   23 *admiral* flagship; *lantern* (which the fleet
follows)   25 *Knight . . . Lamp* i.e. if you were a knight the lamp would be
your emblem   28 *death's-head* skull and crossbones (a pious reminder of
mortality)   29 *Dives* the rich man of the parable in Luke xvi, 19–31   32–33
By . . . angel cf. 'Who [God] maketh his angels spirits, his ministers a
flaming fire' (Psalms civ, 4)

33 God's angel.' But thou art altogether given over, and
wert indeed, but for the light in thy face, the son of utter
darkness. When thou ran'st up Gad's Hill in the night
to catch my horse, if I did not think thou hadst been an
37 ignis fatuus or a ball of wildfire, there's no purchase in
38 money. O, thou art a perpetual triumph, an everlasting
bonfire-light! Thou hast saved me a thousand marks in
40 links and torches, walking with thee in the night betwixt
tavern and tavern; but the sack that thou hast drunk me
42 would have bought me lights as good cheap at the
dearest chandler's in Europe. I have maintained that
44 salamander of yours with fire any time this two-and-
thirty years. God reward me for it!

46 BARDOLPH 'Sblood, I would my face were in your belly!

FALSTAFF God-a-mercy! so should I be sure to be heart-
burnt.

Enter Hostess.

49 How now, Dame Partlet the hen? Have you enquired
yet who picked my pocket?

HOSTESS Why, Sir John, what do you think, Sir John?
Do you think I keep thieves in my house? I have
searched, I have enquired, so has my husband, man by
54 man, boy by boy, servant by servant. The tithe of a hair
was never lost in my house before.

FALSTAFF Ye lie, hostess. Bardolph was shaved and lost
many a hair, and I'll be sworn my pocket was picked.
58 Go to, you are a woman, go!

HOSTESS Who, I? No; I defy thee! God's light, I was
never called so in mine own house before!

FALSTAFF Go to, I know you well enough.

HOSTESS No, Sir John; you do not know me, Sir John. I
know you, Sir John. You owe me money, Sir John, and

---

33 *given over* abandoned as a reprobate   37 *ignis fatuus* will-o'-the-wisp;
wildfire fireworks   38 *triumph* torchlight parade   40 *links* torches   42 *as
good cheap* as cheap   44 *salamander* lizard reputed to live in fire   46 *in your
belly* i.e. rather than on your tongue   49 *Dame Partlet* hen in animal stories
54 *tithe* tenth part   58 *Go to* go on

now you pick a quarrel to beguile me of it. I bought you
a dozen of shirts to your back.

FALSTAFF Dowlas, filthy dowlas! I have given them away 66
to bakers' wives; they have made bolters of them.   67

HOSTESS Now, as I am a true woman, holland of eight 68
shillings an ell. You owe money here besides, Sir John, 69
for your diet and by-drinkings, and money lent you,
four-and-twenty pound.

FALSTAFF He had his part of it; let him pay.

HOSTESS He? Alas, he is poor; he hath nothing.

FALSTAFF How? Poor? Look upon his face. What call
you rich? Let them coin his nose, let them coin his
cheeks. I'll not pay a denier. What, will you make a 76
younker of me? Shall I not take mine ease in mine inn 77
but I shall have my pocket picked? I have lost a seal-
ring of my grandfather's worth forty mark.

HOSTESS O Jesu, I have heard the prince tell him, I know
not how oft, that that ring was copper!

FALSTAFF How? the prince is a Jack, a sneak-up. 82
'Sblood, an he were here, I would cudgel him like a dog
if he would say so.   84

*Enter the Prince [and Peto], marching, and Falstaff
meets them, playing upon his truncheon like a fife.*

How now, lad? Is the wind in that door, i' faith? Must 85
we all march?

BARDOLPH Yea, two and two, Newgate fashion.   87

HOSTESS My lord, I pray you hear me.

PRINCE What say'st thou, Mistress Quickly? How doth
thy husband? I love him well; he is an honest man.

HOSTESS Good my lord, hear me.

FALSTAFF Prithee let her alone and list to me.

PRINCE What say'st thou, Jack?

---

66 *Dowlas* coarse linen   67 *bolters* flour-sifters   68 *holland* fine linen   69
ell measure of forty-five inches   76 *denier* one-twelfth of a sou   77 *younker*
greenhorn, victim   82 *Jack* knave; *sneak-up* sneak   84 s.d. *truncheon*
officer's stick   85 *in that door* in that quarter   87 *Newgate fashion* chained
together (like inmates of Newgate prison)

FALSTAFF The other night I fell asleep here behind the
arras and had my pocket picked. This house is turned
bawdy house; they pick pockets.

PRINCE What didst thou lose, Jack?

FALSTAFF Wilt thou believe me, Hal, three or four bonds
of forty pound apiece and a seal-ring of my grandfather's.

100 PRINCE A trifle, some eightpenny matter.

HOSTESS So I told him, my lord, and I said I heard your
grace say so; and, my lord, he speaks most vilely of you,
like a foulmouthed man as he is, and said he would
cudgel you.

PRINCE What! he did not?

HOSTESS There's neither faith, truth, nor womanhood
in me else.

FALSTAFF There's no more faith in thee than in a
108 stewed prune, nor no more truth in thee than in a drawn
109 fox; and for womanhood, Maid Marian may be the
110 deputy's wife of the ward to thee. Go, you thing, go!

HOSTESS Say, what thing? what thing?

FALSTAFF What thing? Why, a thing to thank God on.

HOSTESS I am no thing to thank God on, I would thou
shouldst know it! I am an honest man's wife, and,
setting thy knighthood aside, thou art a knave to call me
so.

FALSTAFF Setting thy womanhood aside, thou art a
beast to say otherwise.

HOSTESS Say, what beast, thou knave, thou?

FALSTAFF What beast? Why, an otter.

PRINCE An otter, Sir John? Why an otter?

FALSTAFF Why? She's neither fish nor flesh; a man
122 knows not where to have her.

HOSTESS Thou art an unjust man in saying so. Thou or

108–09 *drawn fox* driven from cover (therefore tricky)   109 *womanhood*
womanly respectability; *Maid Marian* (disreputable) woman in morris
dances   110 *deputy's wife* i.e. eminently respectable woman; *to* compared
to   122 *where . . . her* what to make of her

any man knows where to have me, thou knave, thou!

PRINCE Thou say'st true, hostess, and he slanders thee most grossly.

HOSTESS So he doth you, my lord, and said this other day you ought him a thousand pound.   128

PRINCE Sirrah, do I owe you a thousand pound?

FALSTAFF A thousand pound, Hal? A million! Thy love is worth a million; thou owest me thy love.

HOSTESS Nay, my lord, he called you Jack and said he would cudgel you.

FALSTAFF Did I, Bardolph?

BARDOLPH Indeed, Sir John, you said so.

FALSTAFF Yea, if he said my ring was copper.

PRINCE I say 'tis copper. Darest thou be as good as thy word now?

FALSTAFF Why, Hal, thou knowest, as thou art but man, I dare; but as thou art prince, I fear thee as I fear the   140
roaring of the lion's whelp.

PRINCE And why not as the lion?

FALSTAFF The king himself is to be feared as the lion. Dost thou think I'll fear thee as I fear thy father? Nay, an I do, I pray God my girdle break.

PRINCE O, if it should, how would thy guts fall about thy knees! But, sirrah, there's no room for faith, truth, nor honesty in this bosom of thine. It is all filled up with guts and midriff. Charge an honest woman with picking thy pocket? Why, thou whoreson, impudent, embossed   150
rascal, if there were anything in thy pocket but tavern   151
reckonings, memorandums of bawdy houses, and one poor pennyworth of sugar candy to make thee long-winded – if thy pocket were enriched with any other injuries but these, I am a villain. And yet you will   155
stand to it; you will not pocket up wrong. Art thou not   156
ashamed?

---

128 *ought* owed   **150** *embossed* swollen   **151** *rascal* (literally) lean deer   **155** *injuries* things the loss of which would injure you   **156** *stand to it* make a stand; *pocket up* endure

FALSTAFF Dost thou hear, Hal? Thou knowest in the state of innocency Adam fell, and what should poor Jack Falstaff do in the days of villainy? Thou seest I have more flesh than another man, and therefore more frailty. You confess then, you picked my pocket?

PRINCE It appears so by the story.

FALSTAFF Hostess, I forgive thee. Go make ready breakfast. Love thy husband, look to thy servants, cherish thy guests. Thou shalt find me tractable to any honest
166   reason. Thou seest I am pacified still. Nay, prithee be gone.   *Exit Hostess.*
Now, Hal, to the news at court. For the robbery, lad – how is that answered?

PRINCE O my sweet beef, I must still be good angel to thee. The money is paid back again.

FALSTAFF O, I do not like that paying back! 'Tis a double labor.

PRINCE I am good friends with my father, and may do anything.

FALSTAFF Rob me the exchequer the first thing thou
176   doest, and do it with unwashed hands too.

BARDOLPH Do, my lord.

178 **PRINCE** I have procured thee, Jack, a charge of foot.

FALSTAFF I would it had been of horse. Where shall I find one that can steal well? O for a fine thief of the age
181   of two-and-twenty or thereabouts! I am heinously unprovided. Well, God be thanked for these rebels. They offend none but the virtuous. I laud them, I praise them.

PRINCE Bardolph!

BARDOLPH My lord?

PRINCE
Go bear this letter to Lord John of Lancaster,
To my brother John; this to my Lord of Westmoreland.
                                                     [Exit Bardolph.]

---

166 *still* always   176 *with unwashed hands* i.e. without delay   178 *charge of foot* infantry command   181 *unprovided* unprepared

Go, Peto, to horse, to horse; for thou and I
Have thirty miles to ride yet ere dinner time.
                                        [Exit Peto.]
Jack, meet me to-morrow in the Temple Hall
At two o'clock in the afternoon.
There shalt thou know thy charge, and there receive
Money and order for their furniture.   193
The land is burning; Percy stands on high;
And either we or they must lower lie.   *[Exit.]*

FALSTAFF

Rare words! brave world! Hostess, my breakfast, come. 196
O, I could wish this tavern were my drum!   *Exit.* 197

*

[Enter Hotspur, Worcester, and Douglas.]   IV, i

HOTSPUR

Well said, my noble Scot. If speaking truth
In this fine age were not thought flattery,
Such attribution should the Douglas have   3
As not a soldier of this season's stamp
Should go so general current through the world.   5
By God, I cannot flatter, I do defy   6
The tongues of soothers! but a braver place   7
In my heart's love hath no man than yourself.
Nay, task me to my word; approve me, lord.   9

DOUGLAS

Thou art the king of honor.
No man so potent breathes upon the ground
But I will beard him.   12
        Enter one with letters.

HOTSPUR   Do so, and 'tis well. —

193 *furniture* equipment   196 *brave* splendid   197 *tavern* (1) inn, (2) drum
called 'tabor' or 'taborn'; *drum* (which leads soldiers into battle)
IV, i The rebel camp at Shrewsbury   3 *attribution* tribute   5 *go . . . current*
be so universally honored   6 *defy* despise   7 *soothers* flatterers; *braver*
better   9 *task* challenge; *approve* put to the test   12 *But* but that; *beard* defy

What letters hast thou there? – I can but thank you.
MESSENGER
These letters come from your father.
HOTSPUR
Letters from him? Why comes he not himself?
MESSENGER
He cannot come, my lord; he is grievous sick.
HOTSPUR
Zounds! how has he the leisure to be sick
18   In such a justling time? Who leads his power?
Under whose government come they along?
MESSENGER
His letters bears his mind, not I, my lord.
WORCESTER
I prithee tell me, doth he keep his bed?
MESSENGER
He did, my lord, four days ere I set forth,
And at the time of my departure thence
24   He was much feared by his physicians.
WORCESTER
25   I would the state of time had first been whole
Ere he by sickness had been visited.
His health was never better worth than now.
HOTSPUR
Sick now? droop now? This sickness doth infect
The very lifeblood of our enterprise.
'Tis catching hither, even to our camp.
He writes me here that inward sickness –
32   And that his friends by deputation could not
33   So soon be drawn; nor did he think it meet
To lay so dangerous and dear a trust
35   On any soul removed but on his own.
36   Yet doth he give us bold advertiscment,
37   That with our small conjunction we should on,

18 *justling* turbulent   24 *feared* feared for   25 *time* the times   32 *deputation* deputies   33 *drawn* assembled   35 *removed but* i.e. other than   36 *advertisement* advice   37 *conjunction* united force; *on* go on

To see how fortune is disposed to us;
For, as he writes, there is no quailing now,
Because the king is certainly possessed   40
Of all our purposes. What say you to it?

WORCESTER
Your father's sickness is a maim to us.

HOTSPUR
A perilous gash, a very limb lopped off.
And yet, in faith, it is not! His present want
Seems more than we shall find it. Were it good
To set the exact wealth of all our states   46
All at one cast? to set so rich a main   47
On the nice hazard of one doubtful hour?   48
It were not good; for therein should we read   49
The very bottom and the soul of hope,   50
The very list, the very utmost bound   51
Of all our fortunes.

DOUGLAS   Faith, and so we should.
Where now remains a sweet reversion,   53
We may boldly spend upon the hope of what
Is to come in.
A comfort of retirement lives in this.

HOTSPUR
A rendezvous, a home to fly unto,
If that the devil and mischance look big   58
Upon the maidenhead of our affairs.   59

WORCESTER
But yet I would your father had been here.
The quality and hair of our attempt   61
Brooks no division. It will be thought   62
By some that know not why he is away,
That wisdom, loyalty, and mere dislike   64
Of our proceedings kept the earl from hence.

---

40 *possessed* informed   **46** *states* estates   **47** *main* stake   **48** *hazard* (1) peril, (2) dice game   **49** *read* learn   **50** *soul* (1) essence, (2) sole   **51** *list* limit   **53** *reversion* future prospects   **58** *big* threatening   **59** *maidenhead* early phase   **61** *hair* nature   **62** *Brooks* tolerates   **64** *mere* utter

And think how such an apprehension
67   May turn the tide of fearful faction
And breed a kind of question in our cause.
For well you know we of the off'ring side
70   Must keep aloof from strict arbitrement,
71   And stop all sight-holes, every loop from whence
The eye of reason may pry in upon us.
73   This absence of your father's draws a curtain
That shows the ignorant a kind of fear
Before not dreamt of.
75 HOTSPUR   You strain too far.
I rather of his absence make this use:
77   It lends a lustre and more great opinion,
A larger dare to our great enterprise,
Than if the earl were here; for men must think,
80   If we, without his help, can make a head
To push against a kingdom, with his help
We shall o'erturn it topsy-turvy down.
Yet all goes well; yet all our joints are whole.

DOUGLAS
As heart can think. There is not such a word
Spoke of in Scotland as this term of fear.
        Enter Sir Richard Vernon.

HOTSPUR
My cousin Vernon! welcome, by my soul.

VERNON
Pray God my news be worth a welcome, lord.
The Earl of Westmoreland, seven thousand strong,
Is marching hitherwards; with him Prince John.

HOTSPUR
No harm. What more?

VERNON   And further, I have learned
The king himself in person is set forth,
92   Or hitherwards intended speedily,

---

67 *fearful* timid; *faction* conspiracy 70 *arbitrement* scrutiny 71 *loop*
loophole 73 *draws* opens 75 *strain* exaggerate 77 *opinion* prestige 80
make a head raise a force 92 *intended* intended to come

With strong and mighty preparation.

HOTSPUR
He shall be welcome too. Where is his son,
The nimble-footed madcap Prince of Wales,
And his comrades, that daffed the world aside   96
And bid it pass?   97
VERNON   All furnished, all in arms;
All plumed like estridges that with the wind   98
Bated like eagles having lately bathed;   99
Glittering in golden coats like images;
As full of spirit as the month of May
And gorgeous as the sun at midsummer;
Wanton as youthful goats, wild as young bulls.   103
I saw young Harry with his beaver on,   104
His cushes on his thighs, gallantly armed,   105
Rise from the ground like feathered Mercury,
And vaulted with such ease into his seat
As if an angel dropped down from the clouds
To turn and wind a fiery Pegasus   109
And witch the world with noble horsemanship.   110

HOTSPUR
No more, no more! Worse than the sun in March,
This praise doth nourish agues. Let them come.   112
They come like sacrifices in their trim,   113
And to the fire-eyed maid of smoky war   114
All hot and bleeding will we offer them.
The mailèd Mars shall on his altar sit
Up to the ears in blood. I am on fire
To hear this rich reprisal is so nigh,   118
And yet not ours. Come, let me taste my horse,   119

96 *daffed* thrust   97 *bid it pass* refused to take it seriously; *furnished* fitted out   98 *estridges* ostriches   99 *Bated* fluttered their wings   103 *Wanton* sportive   104 *beaver* i.e. helmet   105 *cushes* armor for the thighs   109 *wind* wheel; *Pegasus* i.e. mettlesome horse (literally, the winged horse of Greek mythology)   110 *witch* charm   112 *agues* (attributed to vapors drawn up by the sun)   113 *trim* decorations   114 *maid* the goddess Bellona   118 *reprisal* prize   119 *taste* feel

Who is to bear me like a thunderbolt
Against the bosom of the Prince of Wales.
Harry to Harry shall, hot horse to horse,
Meet, and ne'er part till one drop down a corse.
O that Glendower were come!

VERNON   There is more news.
I learned in Worcester, as I rode along,
126   He cannot draw his power this fourteen days.

DOUGLAS
That's the worst tidings that I hear of yet.

WORCESTER
Ay, by my faith, that bears a frosty sound.

HOTSPUR
129   What may the king's whole battle reach unto?

VERNON
To thirty thousand.

HOTSPUR   Forty let it be.
My father and Glendower being both away,
The powers of us may serve so great a day.
Come, let us take a muster speedily.
Doomsday is near. Die all, die merrily.

DOUGLAS
135   Talk not of dying. I am out of fear
Of death or death's hand for this one half-year.   *Exeunt.*

*

IV, ii   *Enter Falstaff and Bardolph.*

FALSTAFF Bardolph, get thee before to Coventry; fill me
a bottle of sack. Our soldiers shall march through. We'll
to Sutton Co'fil' to-night.

BARDOLPH Will you give me money, captain?

5 FALSTAFF Lay out, lay out.

6 BARDOLPH This bottle makes an angel.

---

126 *draw* muster   129 *battle* army   135 *out of* free from
IV, ii The road to Coventry   5 *Lay out* put up the money yourself   6
angel 10 shillings

FALSTAFF An if it do, take it for thy labor; an if it make 7
twenty, take them all; I'll answer the coinage. Bid my 8
lieutenant Peto meet me at town's end.

BARDOLPH I will, captain. Farewell. *Exit.*

FALSTAFF If I be not ashamed of my soldiers, I am a
soused gurnet. I have misused the king's press dam- 12
nably. I have got, in exchange of a hundred and fifty 13
soldiers, three hundred and odd pounds. I press me 14
none but good householders, yeomen's sons; inquire
me out contracted bachelors, such as had been asked
twice on the banes – such a commodity of warm slaves 17
as had as lieve hear the devil as a drum, such as fear the
report of a caliver worse than a struck fowl or a hurt 19
wild duck. I pressed me none but such toasts-and-
butter, with hearts in their bellies no bigger than pins'
heads, and they have bought out their services; and 22
now my whole charge consists of ancients, corporals, 23
lieutenants, gentlemen of companies – slaves as ragged 24
as Lazarus in the painted cloth, where the glutton's 25
dogs licked his sores; and such as indeed were never
soldiers, but discarded unjust servingmen, younger 27
sons to younger brothers, revolted tapsters, and 28
ostlers trade-fall'n; the cankers of a calm world and a 29
long peace; ten times more dishonorable ragged than an
old fazed ancient; and such have I to fill up the rooms of 30
them as have bought out their services that you would

---

7 *An . . . do* (Falstaff pretends that Bardolph speaks of coining angels) 8
answer be responsible for 12 *soused gurnet* pickled fish; *press* right of
conscription 13 *in exchange of* i.e. for letting off (150 conscripts) 14 *press*
draft 17 *banes* banns (public announcement of intent to marry, made three
times); *warm* well-to-do 19 *caliver* musket 22 *bought . . . services* i.e.
bribed me to let them stay at home 23 *charge* company; *ancients* ensigns
(Falstaff has signed on a disproportionate number of his recruits as officers
in order to collect, and appropriate, their higher pay) 24 *gentlemen of
companies* gentlemen volunteers 25 *Lazarus* the beggar in the parable
(Luke xvi, 19–31); *painted cloth* wall-hangings 27 *unjust* dishonest 28
revolted runaway 29 *trade-fall'n* out of work; *cankers* cankerworms
30 *fazed ancient* frayed flag

think that I had a hundred and fifty tattered prodigals
33 lately come from swine-keeping, from eating draff and
husks. A mad fellow met me on the way, and told me I
had unloaded all the gibbets and pressed the dead
bodies. No eye hath seen such scarecrows. I'll not
march through Coventry with them, that's flat. Nay,
and the villains march wide betwixt the legs, as if they
had gyves on, for indeed I had the most of them out of
prison. There's not a shirt and a half in all my company,
and the half-shirt is two napkins tacked together and
thrown over the shoulders like a herald's coat without
sleeves; and the shirt, to say the truth, stol'n from my
host at Saint Alban's, or the red-nose innkeeper of
Daventry. But that's all one; they'll find linen enough
on every hedge.

Enter the Prince and the Lord of Westmoreland.

PRINCE How now, blown Jack? How now, quilt?

FALSTAFF What, Hal? How now, mad wag? What a devil
dost thou in Warwickshire? My good Lord of West-
49 moreland, I cry you mercy. I thought your honor had
already been at Shrewsbury.

WESTMORELAND Faith, Sir John, 'tis more than time
that I were there, and you too, but my powers are there
already. The king, I can tell you, looks for us all. We
54 must away all night.

55 FALSTAFF Tut, never fear me: I am as vigilant as a cat to
steal cream.

PRINCE I think, to steal cream indeed, for thy theft hath
already made thee butter. But tell me, Jack, whose
fellows are these that come after?

FALSTAFF Mine, Hal, mine.

PRINCE I did never see such pitiful rascals.

62 FALSTAFF Tut, tut! good enough to toss; food for
powder, food for powder. They'll fill a pit as well as

---

33 *draff* garbage   49 *cry you mercy* beg your pardon   54 *must away* must
march   55 *fear* worry about; *vigilant* wakeful   62 *toss* i.e. on a pike

better. Tush, man, mortal men, mortal men.

WESTMORELAND Ay, but, Sir John, methinks they are exceeding poor and bare – too beggarly.

FALSTAFF Faith, for their poverty, I know not where they had that, and for their bareness, I am sure they never learned that of me.

PRINCE No, I'll be sworn, unless you call three fingers in the ribs bare. But, sirrah, make haste. Percy is already in the field.   *Exit*.

FALSTAFF What, is the king encamped?

WESTMORELAND He is, Sir John. I fear we shall stay too long.   *[Exit.]*

FALSTAFF Well, to the latter end of a fray and the beginning of a feast fits a dull fighter and a keen guest.

                                                                            Exit.

*

Enter Hotspur, Worcester, Douglas, Vernon.   IV, iii

HOTSPUR
We'll fight with him to-night.

WORCESTER   It may not be.

DOUGLAS
You give him then advantage.

VERNON   Not a whit.

HOTSPUR
Why say you so? Looks he not for supply?   3

VERNON
So do we.

HOTSPUR His is certain, ours is doubtful.

WORCESTER
Good cousin, be advised; stir not to-night.   5

VERNON
Do not, my lord.

DOUGLAS   You do not counsel well.

IV, iii The rebel camp   3 *supply* reinforcements   5 *be advised* listen to reason

You speak it out of fear and cold heart.

VERNON
Do me no slander, Douglas. By my life –
And I dare well maintain it with my life –
10   If well-respected honor bid me on,
I hold as little counsel with weak fear
As you, my lord, or any Scot that this day lives.
Let it be seen to-morrow in the battle
Which of us fears.

DOUGLAS   Yea, or to-night.

VERNON   Content.

HOTSPUR
To-night, say I.

VERNON
Come, come, it may not be. I wonder much,
17   Being men of such great leading as you are,
That you foresee not what impediments
19   Drag back our expedition. Certain horse
Of my cousin Vernon's are not yet come up.
Your uncle Worcester's horse came but to-day;
22   And now their pride and mettle is asleep,
Their courage with hard labor tame and dull,
That not a horse is half the half of himself.

HOTSPUR
So are the horses of the enemy
26   In general journey-bated and brought low.
The better part of ours are full of rest.

WORCESTER
The number of the king exceedeth ours.
For God's sake, cousin, stay till all come in.
The trumpet sounds a parley.
Enter Sir Walter Blunt.

BLUNT
I come with gracious offers from the king,

---

10 *well-respected* well-considered   **17** *leading* leadership   **19** *expedition*
progress   **22** *pride* mettle   **26** *journey-bated* wearied

If you vouchsafe me hearing and respect.   31
HOTSPUR
   Welcome, Sir Walter Blunt, and would to God
   You were of our determination.   33
   Some of us love you well; and even those some
   Envy your great deservings and good name,
   Because you are not of our quality,   36
   But stand against us like an enemy.

BLUNT
   And God defend but still I should stand so,   38
   So long as out of limit and true rule   39
   You stand against anointed majesty.
   But to my charge. The king hath sent to know
   The nature of your griefs, and whereupon
   You conjure from the breast of civil peace   43
   Such bold hostility, teaching his duteous land
   Audacious cruelty. If that the king
   Have any way your good deserts forgot,
   Which he confesseth to be manifold,
   He bids you name your griefs, and with all speed
   You shall have your desires with interest,
   And pardon absolute for yourself and these
   Herein misled by your suggestion.   51
HOTSPUR
   The king is kind, and well we know the king
   Knows at what time to promise, when to pay.
   My father and my uncle and myself
   Did give him that same royalty he wears;
   And when he was not six-and-twenty strong,
   Sick in the world's regard, wretched and low,
   A poor unminded outlaw sneaking home,
   My father gave him welcome to the shore;
   And when he heard him swear and vow to God

31 *respect* attention   33 *determination* mind   36 *quality* party   38 *defend*
forbid   39 *rule* conduct   43 *civil* orderly   51 *suggestion* instigation

He came but to be Duke of Lancaster,
62   To sue his livery and beg his peace,
With tears of innocency and terms of zeal,
My father, in kind heart and pity moved,
Swore him assistance, and performed it too.
Now when the lords and barons of the realm
Perceived Northumberland did lean to him,
68   The more and less came in with cap and knee;
Met him in boroughs, cities, villages,
70   Attended him on bridges, stood in lanes,
Laid gifts before him, proffered him their oaths,
Gave him their heirs as pages, followed him
73   Even at the heels in golden multitudes.
74   He presently, as greatness knows itself,
Steps me a little higher than his vow
76   Made to my father, while his blood was poor,
Upon the naked shore at Ravenspurgh;
78   And now, forsooth, takes on him to reform
79   Some certain edicts and some strait decrees
That lie too heavy on the commonwealth;
81   Cries out upon abuses, seems to weep
82   Over his country's wrongs; and by this face,
This seeming brow of justice, did he win
The hearts of all that he did angle for;
85   Proceeded further – cut me off the heads
Of all the favorites that the absent king
87   In deputation left behind him here
When he was personal in the Irish war.

BLUNT
Tut! I came not to hear this.

---

62 *sue his livery* sue as heir for his inheritance   **68** *more and less* great and small   **70** *stood in lanes* lined the roads   **73** *golden* richly dressed   **74** *knows itself* feels its own strength   **76** *blood* spirit   **78** *forsooth* (ironical)   **79** *strait* strict   **81** *Cries out upon* denounces   **82** *face* pretext   **85** *cut . . . heads* (see *Richard II*, III, i); *me* (ethical dative)   **87** *In deputation* as deputies

HOTSPUR   Then to the point.
  In short time after, he deposed the king;
  Soon after that deprived him of his life;
  And in the neck of that tasked the whole state;   92
  To make that worse, suff'red his kinsman March
  (Who is, if every owner were well placed,
  Indeed his king) to be engaged in Wales,   95
  There without ransom to lie forfeited;
  Disgraced me in my happy victories,   97
  Sought to entrap me by intelligence;   98
  Rated mine uncle from the council board;   99
  In rage dismissed my father from the court;
  Broke oath on oath, committed wrong on wrong;
  And in conclusion drove us to seek out
  This head of safety, and withal to pry   103
  Into his title, the which we find
  Too indirect for long continuance.
BLUNT
  Shall I return this answer to the king?
HOTSPUR
  Not so, Sir Walter. We'll withdraw awhile.
  Go to the king; and let there be impawned   108
  Some surety for a safe return again,
  And in the morning early shall mine uncle
  Bring him our purposes; and so farewell.
BLUNT
  I would you would accept of grace and love.
HOTSPUR
  And may be so we shall.
BLUNT   Pray God you do.   *Exeunt.*

*

92 *in the neck of* immediately after; *tasked* taxed 95 *engaged* held as hostage
97 *happy* fortunate 98 *intelligence* espionage 99 *Rated* scolded 103
head army; *withal* at the same time 108 *impawned* pledged

IV, iv   *Enter the Archbishop of York and Sir Michael.*

ARCHBISHOP

1 Hie, good Sir Michael; bear this sealèd brief

2 With wingèd haste to the lord marshal;

3 This to my cousin Scroop; and all the rest

To whom they are directed. If you knew

How much they do import, you would make haste.

SIR MICHAEL

My good lord,

I guess their tenor.

ARCHBISHOP   Like enough you do.

To-morrow, good Sir Michael, is a day

Wherein the fortune of ten thousand men

10 Must bide the touch; for, sir, at Shrewsbury,

As I am truly given to understand,

The king with mighty and quick-raisèd power

Meets with Lord Harry; and I fear, Sir Michael,

What with the sickness of Northumberland,

15 Whose power was in the first proportion,

And what with Owen Glendower's absence thence,

17 Who with them was a rated sinew too

And comes not in, overruled by prophecies –

I fear the power of Percy is too weak

20 To wage an instant trial with the king.

SIR MICHAEL

Why, my good lord, you need not fear;

There is Douglas and Lord Mortimer.

ARCHBISHOP

No, Mortimer is not there.

SIR MICHAEL

But there is Mordake, Vernon, Lord Harry Percy,

IV, iv The palace of the Archbishop of York   1 *brief* letter   2 *lord marshal*
Thomas Mowbray, son of the Duke of Norfolk (*Richard II*, I, i, iii), an
inveterate enemy of the king   3 *Scroop* possibly Lord Scroop of Masham,
the archbishop's nephew, later executed for treason (*Henry V*, II, ii)   10
bide the touch withstand the test (touchstone)   15 *proportion* magnitude
17 *rated sinew* mainstay they counted on   20 *wage* risk; *instant* immediate

And there is my Lord of Worcester, and a head   25
Of gallant warriors, noble gentlemen.

ARCHBISHOP
And so there is; but yet the king hath drawn
The special head of all the land together –
The Prince of Wales, Lord John of Lancaster,
The noble Westmoreland and warlike Blunt,
And many moe corrivals and dear men   31
Of estimation and command in arms.

SIR MICHAEL
Doubt not, my lord, they shall be well opposed.

ARCHBISHOP
I hope no less, yet needful 'tis to fear;
And, to prevent the worst, Sir Michael, speed.
For if Lord Percy thrive not, ere the king   36
Dismiss his power, he means to visit us,
For he hath heard of our confederacy,   38
And 'tis but wisdom to make strong against him.
Therefore make haste. I must go write again
To other friends; and so farewell, Sir Michael.   *Exeunt.*

*

Enter the King, Prince of Wales, Lord John of   V, i
Lancaster, Sir Walter Blunt, Falstaff.

KING
How bloodily the sun begins to peer
Above yon bulky hill! The day looks pale
At his distemp'rature.   3

PRINCE   The southern wind
Doth play the trumpet to his purposes   4
And by his hollow whistling in the leaves
Foretells a tempest and a blust'ring day.

---

25 *head* force   31 *moe* more; *corrivals* partners, allies   36 *thrive* succeed
38 *confederacy* conspiracy
V, i The royal camp at Shrewsbury   3 *distemp'rature* unhealthy appearance
4 *trumpet* trumpeter

KING

7   Then with the losers let it sympathize,

8   For nothing can seem foul to those that win.
        The trumpet sounds. Enter Worcester [and Vernon].
     How now, my Lord of Worcester? 'Tis not well
     That you and I should meet upon such terms
     As now we meet. You have deceived our trust
     And made us doff our easy robes of peace
     To crush our old limbs in ungentle steel.
     This is not well, my lord; this is not well.
     What say you to it? Will you again unknit
     This churlish knot of all-abhorrèd war,

17   And move in that obedient orb again
     Where you did give a fair and natural light,

19   And be no more an exhaled meteor,
     A prodigy of fear, and a portent
     Of broachèd mischief to the unborn times?

WORCESTER

     Hear me, my liege.
     For mine own part, I could be well content

24   To entertain the lag-end of my life
     With quiet hours, for I do protest

26   I have not sought the day of this dislike.

KING

     You have not sought it! How comes it then?

FALSTAFF

     Rebellion lay in his way, and he found it.

PRINCE

29   Peace, chewet, peace!

WORCESTER

     It pleased your majesty to turn your looks
     Of favor from myself and all our house;

32   And yet I must remember you, my lord,

---

7 *sympathize* accord   8 *foul* i.e. foul weather   17 *obedient orb* orb of
obedience   19 *exhaled meteor* vapor drawn up by the sun (visible as streaks
of light), regarded as an omen (*prodigy*)   24 *entertain* occupy, while away
26 *dislike* discord   29 *chewet* chatterer   32 *remember* remind

We were the first and dearest of your friends.
For you my staff of office did I break
In Richard's time, and posted day and night   35
To meet you on the way and kiss your hand
When yet you were in place and in account
Nothing so strong and fortunate as I.
It was myself, my brother, and his son
That brought you home and boldly did outdare   40
The dangers of the time. You swore to us,
And you did swear that oath at Doncaster,
That you did nothing purpose 'gainst the state,
Nor claim no further than your new-fall'n right,   44
The seat of Gaunt, dukedom of Lancaster.
To this we swore our aid. But in short space
It rained down fortune show'ring on your head,
And such a flood of greatness fell on you –
What with our help, what with the absent king,
What with the injuries of a wanton time,   50
The seeming sufferances that you had borne,   51
And the contrarious winds that held the king
So long in his unlucky Irish wars
That all in England did repute him dead –
And from this swarm of fair advantages
You took occasion to be quickly wooed
To gripe the general sway into your hand;   57
Forgot your oath to us at Doncaster;
And, being fed by us, you used us so
As that ungentle gull, the cuckoo's bird,   60
Useth the sparrow – did oppress our nest;
Grew by our feeding to so great a bulk
That even our love durst not come near your sight
For fear of swallowing; but with nimble wing
We were enforced for safety sake to fly
Out of your sight and raise this present head;   66

35 *posted* rode at top speed   40 *outdare* defy   44 *new-fall'n* lately
inherited   50 *injuries* evils; *wanton* disordered   51 *sufferances* sufferings
57 *gripe* seize   60 *ungentle* rude; *gull* unfledged bird   66 *head* armed force

Whereby we stand opposèd by such means
As you yourself have forged against yourself
69 By unkind usage, dangerous countenance,
70 And violation of all faith and troth
Sworn to us in your younger enterprise.

KING

72 These things, indeed, you have articulate,
Proclaimed at market crosses, read in churches,
74 To face the garment of rebellion
75 With some fine color that may please the eye
76 Of fickle changelings and poor discontents,
Which gape and rub the elbow at the news
Of hurlyburly innovation.
And never yet did insurrection want
80 Such water colors to impaint his cause,
Nor moody beggars, starving for a time
Of pell-mell havoc and confusion.

PRINCE

In both your armies there is many a soul
Shall pay full dearly for this encounter,
If once they join in trial. Tell your nephew
The Prince of Wales doth join with all the world
87 In praise of Henry Percy. By my hopes,
88 This present enterprise set off his head,
I do not think a braver gentleman,
More active-valiant or more valiant-young,
More daring or more bold, is now alive
To grace this latter age with noble deeds.
For my part, I may speak it to my shame,
I have a truant been to chivalry;
And so I hear he doth account me too.
Yet this before my father's majesty –
I am content that he shall take the odds

---

69 *dangerous* threatening   70 *troth* truth   72 *articulate* specified   74 *face* trim   75 *color* i.e. excuse   76 *changelings* turncoats   80 *water colors* i.e. thin pretexts   87 *hopes* i.e. of salvation   88 *set . . . head* not charged to his account

Of his great name and estimation,   98
And will, to save the blood on either side,
Try fortune with him in a single fight.

KING

And, Prince of Wales, so dare we venture thee,   101
Albeit considerations infinite   102
Do make against it. No, good Worcester, no!
We love our people well; even those we love
That are misled upon your cousin's part;
And, will they take the offer of our grace,
Both he, and they, and you, yea, every man
Shall be my friend again, and I'll be his.
So tell your cousin, and bring me word
What he will do. But if he will not yield,
Rebuke and dread correction wait on us,   111
And they shall do their office. So be gone.
We will not now be troubled with reply.
We offer fair; take it advisedly.

              Exit Worcester [with Vernon].

PRINCE

It will not be accepted, on my life.
The Douglas and the Hotspur both together
Are confident against the world in arms.

KING

Hence, therefore, every leader to his charge;
For, on their answer, will we set on them,
And God befriend us as our cause is just!

              Exeunt. Manent Prince, Falstaff.

FALSTAFF Hal, if thou see me down in the battle and
bestride me, so! 'Tis a point of friendship.   122

PRINCE Nothing but a colossus can do thee that friendship. Say thy prayers, and farewell.   124

FALSTAFF I would 'twere bedtime, Hal, and all well.

PRINCE Why, thou owest God a death.   *[Exit.]*

---

98 *estimation* reputation   101 *dare* would dare   102 *Albeit* were it not that
111 *wait* attend   122 *so* good   124 *Say thy prayers* prepare for death

FALSTAFF 'Tis not due yet: I would be loath to pay him
before his day. What need I be so forward with him that
129 calls not on me? Well, 'tis no matter; honor pricks me
130 on. Yea, but how if honor prick me off when I come on?
131 How then? Can honor set to a leg? No. Or an arm? No.
Or take away the grief of a wound? No. Honor hath no
skill in surgery then? No. What is honor? A word. What
is that word honor? Air – a trim reckoning! Who hath
it? He that died a Wednesday. Doth he feel it? No. Doth
136 he hear it? No. 'Tis insensible then? Yea, to the dead.
But will it not live with the living? No. Why? Detrac-
tion will not suffer it. Therefore I'll none of it. Honor is
139 a mere scutcheon – and so ends my catechism.   *Exit*.

*

V, ii   *Enter Worcester and Sir Richard Vernon.*

WORCESTER
O no, my nephew must not know, Sir Richard,
The liberal and kind offer of the king.

VERNON
'Twere best he did.

WORCESTER   Then are we all undone.
It is not possible, it cannot be,
The king should keep his word in loving us.
6 He will suspect us still and find a time
To punish this offense in other faults.
8 Supposition all our lives shall be stuck full of eyes;
For treason is but trusted like the fox,
Who, ne'er so tame, so cherished and locked up,
11 Will have a wild trick of his ancestors.
Look how we can, or sad or merrily,

---

129 *calls . . . me* doesn't demand payment   130 *prick me off* check me off
131 *set to* graft on   136 *insensible* imperceptible to the senses   139 *scutcheon*
coat of arms borne at a funeral
V, ii The battlefield at Shrewsbury   6 *still* constantly   8 *Supposition*
suspicious conjecture   11 *wild trick* trait of wildness

Interpretation will misquote our looks,
And we shall feed like oxen at a stall,
The better cherished still the nearer death.   15
My nephew's trespass may be well forgot;
It hath the excuse of youth and heat of blood,
And an adopted name of privilege –
A hare-brained Hotspur, governed by a spleen.   19
All his offenses live upon my head
And on his father's. We did train him on;   21
And, his corruption being ta'en from us,   22
We, as the spring of all, shall pay for all.
Therefore, good cousin, let not Harry know,
In any case, the offer of the king.
   Enter Hotspur [and Douglas].

VERNON
Deliver what you will, I'll say 'tis so.   26
Here comes your cousin.
HOTSPUR   My uncle is returned.
Deliver up my Lord of Westmoreland.
Uncle, what news?
WORCESTER
The king will bid you battle presently.
DOUGLAS
Defy him by the Lord of Westmoreland.
HOTSPUR
Lord Douglas, go you and tell him so.
DOUGLAS
Marry, and shall, and very willingly.   *Exit.*
WORCESTER
There is no seeming mercy in the king.
HOTSPUR
Did you beg any? God forbid!
WORCESTER
I told him gently of our grievances,

15 *cherished* fed   19 *spleen* fiery temper   21 *train* lure   22 *corruption* guilt;
ta'en contracted   26 *Deliver* report

37   Of his oath-breaking, which he mended thus,
38   By now forswearing that he is forsworn.
      He calls us rebels, traitors, and will scourge
      With haughty arms this hateful name in us.
                Enter Douglas.

      DOUGLAS
      Arm, gentlemen! to arms! for I have thrown
42   A brave defiance in King Henry's teeth,
43   And Westmoreland, that was engaged, did bear it;
      Which cannot choose but bring him quickly on.

      WORCESTER
      The Prince of Wales stepped forth before the king
      And, nephew, challenged you to single fight.

      HOTSPUR
      O, would the quarrel lay upon our heads,
      And that no man might draw short breath to-day
      But I and Harry Monmouth! Tell me, tell me,
50   How showed his tasking? Seemed it in contempt?

      VERNON
      No, by my soul. I never in my life
      Did hear a challenge urged more modestly,
      Unless a brother should a brother dare
      To gentle exercise and proof of arms.
55   He gave you all the duties of a man;
56   Trimmed up your praises with a princely tongue;
      Spoke your deservings like a chronicle;
      Making you ever better than his praise
59   By still dispraising praise valued with you;
      And, which became him like a prince indeed,
61   He made a blushing cital of himself,
      And chid his truant youth with such a grace
      As if he mast'red there a double spirit
64   Of teaching and of learning instantly.

37 *mended* made up for   38 *forswearing* denying; *is forsworn* has repudiated
(his oath)   42 *brave* haughty   43 *engaged* held as hostage   50 *tasking* challenge   55 *duties* due merits   56 *Trimmed up* adorned   59 *valued* compared
61 *cital* (1) citation, (2) impeachment   64 *instantly* simultaneously

There did he pause; but let me tell the world,
If he outlive the envy of this day,   66
England did never owe so sweet a hope,   67
So much misconstrued in his wantonness.   68

HOTSPUR
Cousin, I think thou art enamorèd
Upon his follies. Never did I hear
Of any prince so wild a liberty.   71
But be he as he will, yet once ere night
I will embrace him with a soldier's arm,
That he shall shrink under my courtesy.
Arm, arm with speed! and, fellows, soldiers, friends,
Better consider what you have to do
Than I, that have not well the gift of tongue,
Can lift your blood up with persuasion.
        Enter a Messenger.

MESSENGER
My lord, here are letters for you.

HOTSPUR
I cannot read them now. –
O gentlemen, the time of life is short!
To spend that shortness basely were too long
If life did ride upon a dial's point,   83
Still ending at the arrival of an hour.   84
An if we live, we live to tread on kings;
If die, brave death, when princes die with us!   86
Now for our consciences, the arms are fair,
When the intent of bearing them is just.
        Enter another Messenger.

MESSENGER
My lord, prepare. The king comes on apace.

HOTSPUR
I thank him that he cuts me from my tale,
For I profess not talking. Only this –

66 *envy* malice   67 *owe* own   68 *wantonness* sportiveness   71 *liberty*
licentiousness   83 *If* even if; *dial's* clock's   84 *Still . . . hour* i.e. if life were
only an hour long; *Still* inevitably   86 *brave* glorious

123

Let each man do his best; and here draw I
A sword whose temper I intend to stain
With the best blood that I can meet withal
95   In the adventure of this perilous day.
96   Now, Esperancè! Percy! and set on.
Sound all the lofty instruments of war,
And by that music let us all embrace;
For, heaven to earth, some of us never shall
A second time do such a courtesy.

Here they embrace. The trumpets sound.   [Exeunt.]

V, iii   *The King enters with his power. Alarum to the battle.*
[Exeunt.] Then enter Douglas and Sir Walter Blunt.

BLUNT
What is thy name, that in battle thus
Thou crossest me? What honor dost thou seek
Upon my head?

DOUGLAS   Know then my name is Douglas,
And I do haunt thee in the battle thus
Because some tell me that thou art a king.

BLUNT
They tell thee true.

DOUGLAS
The Lord of Stafford dear to-day hath bought
Thy likeness, for instead of thee, King Harry,
This sword hath ended him. So shall it thee,
10   Unless thou yield thee as my prisoner.

BLUNT
I was not born a yielder, thou proud Scot;
And thou shalt find a king that will revenge
Lord Stafford's death.

They fight. Douglas kills Blunt. Then enter Hotspur.

HOTSPUR O Douglas, hadst thou fought at Holmedon
thus, I never had triumphed upon a Scot.

---

95 *adventure* hazard   96 *Esperancè* hope (the Percy battle-cry)
V, iii   s.d. *Alarum* signal to advance

DOUGLAS
All's done, all's won. Here breathless lies the king.

HOTSPUR Where?

DOUGLAS Here.

HOTSPUR
This, Douglas? No. I know this face full well.
A gallant knight he was, his name was Blunt;
Semblably furnished like the king himself.   21

DOUGLAS
A fool go with thy soul, whither it goes!   22
A borrowed title hast thou bought too dear:
Why didst thou tell me that thou wert a king?

HOTSPUR
The king hath many marching in his coats.

DOUGLAS
Now, by my sword, I will kill all his coats;
I'll murder all his wardrobe, piece by piece,
Until I meet the king.

HOTSPUR   Up and away!
Our soldiers stand full fairly for the day.   *Exeunt.* 29
    Alarum. Enter Falstaff solus.

FALSTAFF Though I could scape shot-free at London, I 30
fear the shot here. Here's no scoring but upon the pate. 31
Soft! who are you? Sir Walter Blunt. There's honor for
you! Here's no vanity! I am as hot as molten lead, and as 33
heavy too. God keep lead out of me. I need no more
weight than mine own bowels. I have led my rag-of-
muffins where they are peppered. There's not three of 36
my hundred and fifty left alive, and they are for the
town's end, to beg during life. But who comes here?
    Enter the Prince.

PRINCE
What, stand'st thou idle here? Lend me thy sword.

21 *Semblably furnished* similarly equipped   22 *A . . . soul* i.e. you are a fool
29 *fairly* auspiciously; *day* victory   30 *shot-free* without paying bills   31
scoring (1) cutting, (2) chalking up a debt   33 *Here's no vanity* (ironical)
here's no empty honor   36 *peppered* done for

Many a nobleman lies stark and stiff
Under the hoofs of vaunting enemies,
Whose deaths are yet unrevenged. I prithee
Lend me thy sword.

FALSTAFF O Hal, I prithee give me leave to breathe
45 awhile. Turk Gregory never did such deeds in arms as I
46 have done this day. I have paid Percy; I have made him
sure.

PRINCE
47 He is indeed, and living to kill thee.
I prithee lend me thy sword.

FALSTAFF Nay, before God, Hal, if Percy be alive, thou
get'st not my sword; but take my pistol, if thou wilt.

PRINCE Give it me. What, is it in the case?

FALSTAFF Ay, Hal. 'Tis hot, 'tis hot. There's that will
sack a city.
*The Prince draws it out and finds it to be a bottle of
sack.*

PRINCE
What, is it a time to jest and dally now?
He throws the bottle at him.   *Exit.*

55 FALSTAFF Well, if Percy be alive, I'll pierce him. If he do
come in my way, so; if he do not, if I come in his will-
57 ingly, let him make a carbonado of me. I like not such
grinning honor as Sir Walter hath. Give me life; which
if I can save, so; if not, honor comes unlooked for, and
there's an end.   *Exit.*

V, iv   *Alarum. Excursions. Enter the King, the Prince, Lord
John of Lancaster, Earl of Westmoreland.*

KING
I prithee, Harry, withdraw thyself; thou bleedest too
much.
Lord John of Lancaster, go you with him.

---

45 *Turk Gregory* a ferocious tyrant (invented by Falstaff)   46 *made him sure*
destroyed him   47 *indeed* i.e. sure (safe)   55 *pierce* pronounced 'perce'
57 *carbonado* broiled steak
V, iv   s.d. *Excursions* sorties

JOHN
    Not I, my lord, unless I did bleed too.
PRINCE
    I do beseech your majesty make up,   4
    Lest your retirement do amaze your friends.   5
KING
    I will do so.
    My Lord of Westmoreland, lead him to his tent.
WESTMORELAND
    Come, my lord, I'll lead you to your tent.
PRINCE
    Lead me, my lord? I do not need your help;
    And God forbid a shallow scratch should drive
    The Prince of Wales from such a field as this,
    Where stained nobility lies trodden on,
    And rebels' arms triumph in massacres!
JOHN
    We breathe too long. Come, cousin Westmoreland,
    Our duty this way lies. For God's sake, come.
              [Exeunt Prince John and Westmoreland.]
PRINCE
    By God, thou hast deceived me, Lancaster!
    I did not think thee lord of such a spirit.
    Before, I loved thee as a brother, John;
    But now, I do respect thee as my soul.   19
KING
    I saw him hold Lord Percy at the point
    With lustier maintenance than I did look for   21
    Of such an ungrown warrior.
PRINCE   O, this boy
    Lends mettle to us all!   *Exit.*
        [Enter Douglas.]
DOUGLAS
    Another king? They grow like Hydra's heads.   24

4 *make up* advance   5 *amaze* bewilder   19 *respect* regard   21 *lustier
maintenance* more vigorous bearing   24 *Hydra's heads* (as soon as one was
cut off, two others grew in its place)

I am the Douglas, fatal to all those
That wear those colors on them. What art thou
That counterfeit'st the person of a king?

KING
The king himself, who, Douglas, grieves at heart
29   So many of his shadows thou hast met,
And not the very king. I have two boys
Seek Percy and thyself about the field;
But, seeing thou fall'st on me so luckily,
33   I will assay thee. So defend thyself.

DOUGLAS
I fear thou art another counterfeit;
And yet, in faith, thou bearest thee like a king.
But mine I am sure thou art, whoe'er thou be,
And thus I win thee.
        *They fight. The King being in danger, enter Prince of
        Wales.*

PRINCE
Hold up thy head, vile Scot, or thou art like
Never to hold it up again. The spirits
Of valiant Shirley, Stafford, Blunt are in my arms.
It is the Prince of Wales that threatens thee,
Who never promiseth but he means to pay.
        They fight. Douglas flieth.
43   Cheerly, my lord. How fares your grace?
Sir Nicholas Gawsey hath for succor sent,
And so hath Clifton. I'll to Clifton straight.

KING
Stay and breathe awhile.
47   Thou hast redeemed thy lost opinion,
48   And showed thou mak'st some tender of my life,
In this fair rescue thou hast brought to me.

PRINCE
O God, they did me too much injury

29 *shadows* likenesses   33 *assay* challenge to trial   43 *Cheerly* cheer up
47 *redeemed* regained; *opinion* good name   48 *mak'st some tender of* have
some regard for

That ever said I heark'ned for your death.   51
If it were so, I might have let alone
The insulting hand of Douglas over you,   53
Which would have been as speedy in your end
As all the poisonous potions in the world,
And saved the treacherous labor of your son.

KING
Make up to Clifton; I'll to Sir Nicholas Gawsey.   *Exit.*
          Enter Hotspur.

HOTSPUR
If I mistake not, thou art Harry Monmouth.

PRINCE
Thou speak'st as if I would deny my name.

HOTSPUR
My name is Harry Percy.

PRINCE   Why, then I see
A very valiant rebel of the name.
I am the Prince of Wales, and think not, Percy,
To share with me in glory any more.
Two stars keep not their motion in one sphere,   64
Nor can one England brook a double reign   65
Of Harry Percy and the Prince of Wales.

HOTSPUR
Nor shall it, Harry, for the hour is come
To end the one of us; and would to God
Thy name in arms were now as great as mine!

PRINCE
I'll make it greater ere I part from thee,
And all the budding honors on thy crest   71
I'll crop to make a garland for my head.

HOTSPUR
I can no longer brook thy vanities.   73
          They fight. Enter Falstaff.

FALSTAFF Well said, Hal! to it, Hal! Nay, you shall find   74

---

51 *heark'ned* waited 53 *insulting* exulting 64 *sphere* orbit 65 *brook*
endure 71 *crest* helmet 73 *vanities* boasts 74 *Well said* well done

no boy's play here, I can tell you.
>*Enter Douglas. He fighteth with Falstaff, who falls*
>*down as if he were dead. [Exit Douglas.] The Prince*
>*killeth Percy.*

HOTSPUR
O Harry, thou hast robbed me of my youth!
I better brook the loss of brittle life
Than those proud titles thou hast won of me.
They wound my thoughts worse than thy sword my
    flesh.
80 But thoughts the slaves of life, and life time's fool,
81 And time, that takes survey of all the world,
Must have a stop. O, I could prophesy,
But that the earthy and cold hand of death
Lies on my tongue. No, Percy, thou art dust,
And food for –
    [Dies.]

PRINCE
For worms, brave Percy. Fare thee well, great heart.
Ill-weaved ambition, how much art thou shrunk!
When that this body did contain a spirit,
A kingdom for it was too small a bound;
But now two paces of the vilest earth
Is room enough. This earth that bears thee dead
Bears not alive so stout a gentleman.
93 If thou wert sensible of courtesy,
94 I should not make so dear a show of zeal.
95 But let my favors hide thy mangled face;
And, even in thy behalf, I'll thank myself
For doing these fair rites of tenderness.
Adieu, and take thy praise with thee to heaven.
Thy ignominy sleep with thee in the grave,
But not rememb'red in thy epitaph.

80 *fool* dupe, plaything   81 *takes survey of* oversees   93 *sensible* able to feel
94 *dear* heartfelt; *zeal* admiration   95 *favors* plumes (of his helmet)

He spieth Falstaff on the ground.
What, old acquaintance? Could not all this flesh
Keep in a little life? Poor Jack, farewell!
I could have better spared a better man.
O, I should have a heavy miss of thee   104
If I were much in love with vanity.   105
Death hath not struck so fat a deer to-day,
Though many dearer, in this bloody fray.
Embowelled will I see thee by-and-by;   108
Till then in blood by noble Percy lie.   *Exit.*
    Falstaff riseth up.
FALSTAFF Embowelled? If thou embowel me to-day, I'll
give you leave to powder me and eat me too to-morrow. 111
'Sblood, 'twas time to counterfeit, or that hot termagant 112
Scot had paid me scot and lot too. Counterfeit? I lie; I 113
am no counterfeit. To die is to be a counterfeit, for he is
but the counterfeit of a man who hath not the life of a
man; but to counterfeit dying when a man thereby
liveth, is to be no counterfeit, but the true and perfect
image of life indeed. The better part of valor is discre- 118
tion, in the which better part I have saved my life.
Zounds, I am afraid of this gunpowder Percy, though he
be dead. How if he should counterfeit too, and rise? By
my faith, I am afraid he would prove the better counterfeit. Therefore I'll make him sure; yea, and I'll swear I
killed him. Why may not he rise as well as I? Nothing
confutes me but eyes, and nobody sees me. Therefore,
sirrah *[stabs him]*, with a new wound in your thigh,
come you along with me.
    *He takes up Hotspur on his back. Enter Prince, and
    John of Lancaster.*

104 *have ... thee* (1) miss you sadly, (2) miss something heavy 105 *vanity*
frivolity 108 *Embowelled* eviscerated (the first step in embalming) 111
powder pickle in brine 112 *termagant* violent 113 *scot and lot* i.e. thoroughly 118 *part* quality

PRINCE

128   Come, brother John; full bravely hast thou fleshed
Thy maiden sword.

JOHN   But, soft! whom have we here?
Did you not tell me this fat man was dead?

PRINCE
I did; I saw him dead,
Breathless and bleeding on the ground. Art thou alive,
133   Or is it fantasy that plays upon our eyesight?
I prithee speak. We will not trust our eyes
Without our ears. Thou art not what thou seem'st.

136   **FALSTAFF**   No, that's certain, I am not a double man; but
137   if I be not Jack Falstaff, then am I a Jack. There is
Percy. If your father will do me any honor, so; if not, let
him kill the next Percy himself. I look to be either earl
or duke, I can assure you.

PRINCE   Why, Percy I killed myself, and saw thee dead!

FALSTAFF   Didst thou? Lord, Lord, how this world is
given to lying. I grant you I was down, and out of breath,
and so was he; but we rose both at an instant and fought
a long hour by Shrewsbury clock. If I may be believed,
so; if not, let them that should reward valor bear the sin
upon their own heads. I'll take it upon my death, I gave
him this wound in the thigh. If the man were alive and
would deny it, zounds! I would make him eat a piece of
my sword.

JOHN
This is the strangest tale that ever I heard.

PRINCE
This is the strangest fellow, brother John.
Come, bring your luggage nobly on your back.
153   For my part, if a lie may do thee grace,
I'll gild it with the happiest terms I have.
                    A retreat is sounded.

---

128 *fleshed* initiated   133 *fantasy* hallucination   136 *double man* (1)
spectre, (2) two men   137 *Jack* knave   153 *grace* credit

The trumpet sounds retreat; the day is ours.
Come, brother, let's to the highest of the field,
To see what friends are living, who are dead.
                    Exeunt [Prince Henry and Prince John].
FALSTAFF I'll follow, as they say, for reward. He that re-
wards me, God reward him. If I do grow great, I'll grow
less; for I'll purge, and leave sack, and live cleanly, as a   160
nobleman should do.   *Exit [bearing off the body].*

*

The trumpets sound. Enter the King, Prince of Wales, V, v
Lord John of Lancaster, Earl of Westmoreland, with
Worcester and Vernon prisoners.

KING
Thus ever did rebellion find rebuke.
Ill-spirited Worcester, did not we send grace,   2
Pardon, and terms of love to all of you?
And wouldst thou turn our offers contrary?
Misuse the tenor of thy kinsman's trust?
Three knights upon our party slain to-day,
A noble earl, and many a creature else
Had been alive this hour,
If like a Christian thou hadst truly borne
Betwixt our armies true intelligence.

WORCESTER
What I have done my safety urged me to;
And I embrace this fortune patiently,   12
Since not to be avoided it falls on me.

KING
Bear Worcester to the death, and Vernon too;
Other offenders we will pause upon.
                    [Exeunt Worcester and Vernon, guarded.]
How goes the field?

160 *purge* (1) repent, (2) 'grow less'
V, v The command post of the King   2 *grace* mercy   12 *patiently* with
fortitude

PRINCE

The noble Scot, Lord Douglas, when he saw
The fortune of the day quite turned from him,
The noble Percy slain, and all his men
20 Upon the foot of fear, fled with the rest;
And falling from a hill, he was so bruised
That the pursuers took him. At my tent
The Douglas is, and I beseech your grace
I may dispose of him.

KING   With all my heart.

PRINCE

Then, brother John of Lancaster, to you
26 This honorable bounty shall belong.
Go to the Douglas and deliver him
Up to his pleasure, ransomless and free.
His valors shown upon our crests to-day
Have taught us how to cherish such high deeds,
Even in the bosom of our adversaries.

JOHN

I thank your grace for this high courtesy,
Which I shall give away immediately.

KING

Then this remains, that we divide our power.
You, son John, and my cousin Westmoreland,
36 Towards York shall bend you with your dearest speed
To meet Northumberland and the prelate Scroop,
Who, as we hear, are busily in arms.
Myself and you, son Harry, will towards Wales
To fight with Glendower and the Earl of March.
Rebellion in this land shall lose his sway,
Meeting the check of such another day;
And since this business so fair is done,
44 Let us not leave till all our own be won.   *Exeunt.*

20 *Upon . . . fear* in flight for fear   26 *bounty* benevolence   36 *bend you*
direct yourselves   44 *leave* cease